First published in 1938 by William Collins Sons & Co Ltd
First issued in Fontana Books 1960
Ninth Impression June 1977

© 1937, 1938 by Agatha Christie Mallowan

Made and Printed in Great Britain by
William Collins Sons & Co Ltd Glasgow

L & M

*To Richard and Myra Mallock
to remind them of their
journey to Petra*

CONDITIONS OF SALE:
This book is sold subject to the condition that
it shall not, by way of trade or otherwise, be lent,
re-sold, hired out or otherwise circulated without
the publisher's prior consent in any form of
binding or cover other than that in which it is
published and without a similar condition
including this condition being imposed on the
subsequent purchaser

PART I

Chapter One

" You do see, don't you, that she's got to be killed?"

The question floated out into the still night air, seemed to hang there a moment and then drift away down into the darkness towards the Dead Sea.

Hercule Poirot paused a minute with his hand on the window catch. Frowning, he shut it decisively, thereby excluding any injurious night air! Hercule Poirot had been brought up to believe that all outside air was best left outside, and that night air was especially dangerous to the health.

As he pulled the curtains neatly over the window and walked to his bed, he smiled tolerantly to himself.

" You do see, don't you, that she's got to be killed?"

Curious words for one Hercule Poirot, detective, to overhear on his first night in Jerusalem.

" Decidedly, wherever I go, there is something to remind me of crime!" he murmured to himself.

His smile continued as he remembered a story he had once heard concerning Anthony Trollope the novelist. Trollope was crossing the Atlantic at the time and had overheard two fellow-passengers discussing the last published instalment of one of his novels.

" Very good," one man had declared. " But he ought to kill off that tiresome old woman."

With a broad smile the novelist had addressed them:

" Gentlemen, I am much obliged to you! I will go and kill her immediately!"

Hercule Poirot wondered what had occasioned the words he had just overheard. A collaboration, perhaps, over a play or a book.

He thought, still smiling: " Those words might be remembered, one day, and given a more sinister meaning."

5

There had been, he now recollected, a curious nervous intensity in the voice—a tremor that spoke of some intense emotional strain. A man's voice—or a boy's. . . .

Hercule Poirot thought to himself as he turned out the light by his bed: " *I should know that voice again. . . .*"

Their elbows on the window-sill, their heads close together, Raymond and Carol Boynton gazed out into the blue depths of the night. Nervously, Raymond repeated his former words: " You do see, don't you, that she's got to be killed?"

Carol Boynton stirred slightly. She said, her voice deep and hoarse: " It's horrible. . . ."

" It's not more horrible than *this*!"

" I suppose not. . . ."

Raymond said violently: " It can't go on like this—it can't. . . . We *must* do something. . . . And there isn't anything else we *can* do. . . ."

Carol said—but her voice was unconvincing and she knew it: " If we could get away somehow——?"

" We can't." His voice was empty and hopeless. " Carol, you know we can't. . . ."

The girl shivered. " I know, Ray—I know."

He gave a sudden short, bitter laugh.

" People would say we were crazy—not to be able just to walk out——"

Carol said slowly: " Perhaps we—are crazy!"

" I dare say. Yes, I dare say we are. Anyway, we soon shall be. . . . I suppose some people would say we are already —here we are calmly planning, in cold blood, to kill our own mother!"

Carol said sharply: " She isn't our own mother!"

" No, that's true."

There was a pause and then Raymond said, his voice now quietly matter-of-fact: " You do agree, Carol?"

Carol answered steadily: " I think she ought to die—yes. . . ."

Then she broke out suddenly: " She's mad. . . . I'm quite sure she's mad. . . . She—she couldn't torture us like she does if she were sane. For years we've been saying: ' *This can't go on!*' and it *has* gone on! We've said, ' *She'll die sometime*'— but she hasn't died! I don't think she ever will die unless——"

Raymond said steadily: " *Unless we kill her. . . .*"

" Yes."

6

She clenched her hands on the window-sill in front of her.

Her brother went on in a cool, matter-of-fact tone, with just a slight tremor denoting his deep underlying excitement.

" You see why it's got to be one of us, don't you? With Lennox, there's Nadine to consider. And we couldn't bring Jinny into it."

Carol shivered.

" Poor Jinny. . . . I'm so afraid. . . ."

" I know. It's getting pretty bad, isn't it? That's why something's got to be done quickly—before she goes right over the edge."

Carol stood up suddenly, pushing back the tumbled chestnut hair from her forehead.

" Ray," she said, " you don't think it's really *wrong,* do you?"

He answered in that same would-be dispassionate tone. " No. I think it's just like killing a mad dog—something that's doing harm in the world and must be stopped. This is the only way of stopping it."

Carol murmured: " But they'd—they'd send us to the chair just the same. . . . I mean we couldn't explain what she's like. . . . It would sound fantastic. . . . In a way, you know, it's all in our own *minds* ! "

Raymond said: " Nobody will ever know. I've got a plan. I've thought it all out. We shall be quite safe."

Carol turned suddenly round on him.

" Ray—somehow or another—you're different. Something's *happened* to you. . . . What's put all this into your head?"

" Why should you think anything's happened to me?"

He turned his head away, staring out into the night.

" Because it has. . . . Ray, was it that girl on the train?"

" No, of course not—why should it be? Oh, Carol, don't talk nonsense. Le's get back again to—to——"

" To your plan? Are you sure it's a—good plan?"

" Yes. I think so. . . . We must wait for the right opportunity, of course. And then—if it goes all right—we shall be free —all of us."

" Free?" Carol gave a little sigh. She looked up at the stars. Then suddenly she shook from head to foot in a sudden storm of weeping.

" Carol, what's the matter?"

She sobbed out brokenly: " It's so lovely—the night and the blueness and the stars. If only we could be part of it

7

all. . . . If only we could be like other people instead of being as we are—all queer and warped and *wrong*."

" But we shall be—all right—when she's dead! "

" Are you *sure*? Isn't it too late? Shan't we always be queer and different?"

" No, no, no."

" I wonder——"

" Carol, if you'd rather not——"

She pushed his comforting arm aside.

" No, I'm with you—definitely I'm with you! Because of the others—especially Jinny. We *must* save Jinny! "

Raymond paused a moment. " Then—we'll go on with it?"

" Yes! "

" Good. I'll tell you my plan. . . ."

He bent his head to hers.

Chapter 2

MISS SARAH KING, M.B., stood by the table in the writing-room of the Solomon Hotel in Jerusalem, idly turning over the papers and magazines. A frown contracted her brows and she looked preoccupied.

The tall middle-aged Frenchman who entered the room from the hall watched her for a moment or two before strolling up to the opposite side of the table. When their eyes met, Sarah made a little gesture of smiling recognition. She remembered that this man had come to help her when travelling from Cairo and had carried one of her suitcases at a moment when no porter appeared to be available.

" You like Jerusalem, yes?" asked Dr. Gerard after they had exchanged greetings.

" It's rather terrible in some ways," said Sarah, and added: " Religion is very odd! "

The Frenchman looked amused.

" I know what you mean." His English was very nearly perfect. " Every imaginable sect squabbling and fighting! "

" And the awful things they've built, too! " said Sarah.

" Yes, indeed."

Sarah sighed.

" They turned me out of one place to-day because I had on

8

a sleeveless dress," she said ruefully. "Apparently the Almighty doesn't like my arms in spite of having made them."

Dr. Gerard laughed. Then he said: "I was about to order some coffee. You will join me, Miss——?"

"King, my name is. Sarah King."

"And mine—permit me." He whipped out a card. Taking it, Sarah's eyes widened in delighted awe.

"Dr. Theodore Gerard? Oh! I *am* excited to meet you. I've read all your works, of course. Your views on schizophrenia are frightfully interesting."

"*Of course?*" Gerard's eyebrows rose inquisitively.

Sarah explained rather diffidently.

"You see—I'm by way of being a doctor myself. Just got my M.B."

"Ah! I see."

Dr. Gerard ordered coffee and they sat down in a corner of the lounge. The Frenchman was less interested in Sarah's medical achievements than in the black hair that rippled back from her forehead and the beautifully shaped red mouth. He was amused at the obvious awe with which she regarded him.

"You are staying here long?" he asked conversationally.

"A few days. That is all. Then I want to go to Petra."

"Aha ! I, too, was thinking of going there if it does not take too long. You see, I have to be back in Paris on the fourteenth."

"It takes about a week, I believe. Two days to go, two days there and two days back again."

"I must go to the travel bureau in the morning and see what can be arranged."

A party of people entered the lounge and sat down. Sarah watched them with some interest. She lowered her voice.

"Those people who have just come in, did you notice them on the train the other night? They left Cairo the same time as we did."

Dr. Gerard screwed in an eyeglass and directed his glance across the room. "Americans?"

Sarah nodded.

"Yes. An American family. But—rather an unusual one, I think."

"Unusual? How unusual?"

"Well, look at them. Especially at the old woman."

Dr. Gerard complied. His keen professional glance flitted swiftly from face to face.

He noticed first a tall rather loose-boned man—age about thirty. The face was pleasant but weak and his manner seemed oddly apathetic. Then there were two good-looking youngsters—the boy had almost a Greek head. "Something the matter with him, too," thought Dr. Gerard. "Yes—a definite state of nervous tension." The girl was clearly his sister, a strong resemblance, and she also was in an excitable condition. There was another girl younger still—with golden red hair that stood out like a halo, her hands were very restless, they were tearing and pulling at the handkerchief in her lap. Yet another woman, young, calm, dark-haired with a creamy pallor, a placid face not unlike a Luini Madonna. Nothing jumpy about *her*! And the centre of the group—"Heavens!" thought Dr. Gerard, with a Frenchman's candid repulsion. "What a horror of a woman!" Old, swollen, bloated, sitting there immovable in the midst of them—a distorted old Buddha—a gross spider in the centre of a web!

To Sarah he said: "*La Maman*, she is not beautiful, eh?" And he shrugged his shoulders.

"There's something rather—sinister about her, don't you think?" asked Sarah.

Dr. Gerard scrutinised her again. This time his eye was professional, not æsthetic.

"Dropsy—cardiac——" he added a glib medical phrase.

"Oh, yes, *that*!" Sarah dismissed the medical side.

"But there is something odd in their attitude to her, don't you think?"

"Who are they, do you know?"

"Their name is Boynton. Mother, married son, his wife, one younger son and two younger daughters."

Dr. Gerard murmured: "*La famille Boynton* sees the world."

"Yes, but there's something odd about the *way* they're seeing it. They never speak to anyone else. And none of them can do anything unless the old woman says so!"

"She is of the matriarchal type," said Gerard thoughtfully.

"She's a complete tyrant, I think," said Sarah.

Dr. Gerard shrugged his shoulders and remarked that the American woman ruled the earth—that was well known.

"Yes, but it's more than just that." Sarah was persistent.

10

" She's—oh, she's got them all so *cowed*—so positively under her thumb—that it's—it's indecent!'"

" To have too much power is bad for women," Gerard agreed with sudden gravity. He shook his head.

" It is difficult for a woman not to abuse power."

He shot a quick sideways glance at Sarah. She was watching the Boynton family—or rather she was watching one particular member of it. Dr. Gerard smiled a quick comprehending Gallic smile. Ah! So it was like that, was it?

He murmured tentatively: " You have spoken with them —yes?"

" Yes—at least with one of them."

" The young man—the younger son?"

" Yes. On the train coming here from Kantara. He was standing in the corridor. I spoke to him."

There was no self-consciousness in her attitude to life. She was interested in humanity and was of a friendly though impatient disposition.

" What made you speak to him?" asked Gerard.

Sarah shrugged her shoulders.

" Why not? I often speak to people travelling. I'm interested in people—in what they do and think and feel."

" You put them under the microscope, that is to say."

" I suppose you might call it that," the girl admitted.

" And what were your impressions in this case?"

" Well," she hesitated, " it was rather odd. . . . To begin with, the boy flushed right up to the roots of his hair."

" Is that so remarkable?" asked Gerard dryly.

Sarah laughed.

" You mean that he thought I was a shameless hussy making advances to him? Oh, no, I don't think he thought that. Men can always tell, can't they?"

She gave him a frank questioning glance. Dr. Gerard nodded his head.

" I got the impression," said Sarah, speaking slowly and frowning a little, " that he was—how shall I put it?—both excited and appalled. Excited out of all proportion—and quite absurdly apprehensive at the same time. Now that's odd, isn't it? Because I've always found Americans unusually self-possessed. An American boy of twenty, say, has infinitely more knowledge of the world and far more *savoir-faire* than an English boy of the same age. And this boy must be over twenty."

11

" About twenty-three or four, I should say."

" As much as that?"

" I should think so."

" Yes . . . perhaps you're right. . . . Only, somehow, he seems very young. . . ."

" Maladjustment mentally. The 'child' factor persists."

" Then I *am* right? I mean, there *is* something not quite normal about him?"

Dr. Gerard shrugged his shoulders, smiling a little at her earnestness.

" My dear young lady, are any of us quite normal? But I grant you that there is probably a neurosis of some kind."

" Connected with that horrible old woman, I'm sure."

" You seem to dislike her very much," said Gerard, looking at her curiously.

" I do. She's got a—oh, a malevolent eye!"

Gerard murmured: " So have many mothers when their sons are attracted to fascinating young ladies!"

Sarah shrugged an impatient shoulder. Frenchmen were all alike, she thought, obsessed by sex! Though, of course, as a conscientious psychologist she herself was bound to admit that there was always an underlying basis of sex to most phenomena. Sarah's thoughts ran along a familiar psychological track.

She came out of her meditations with a start. Raymond Boynton was crossing the room to the centre table. He selected a magazine. As he passed her chair on his return journey she looked at him and spoke.

" Have you been busy sightseeing to-day?"

She selected her words at random, her real interest was to see how they would be received.

Raymond half stopped, flushed, shied like a nervous horse and his eyes went apprehensively to the centre of his family group. He muttered: " Oh—oh, yes—why, yes, certainly. I——"

Then, as suddenly as though he had received the prick of a spur, he hurried back to his family, holding out the magazine.

The grotesque Buddha-like figure held out a fat hand for it, but as she took it her eyes, Dr. Gerard noticed, were on the boy's face. She gave a grunt, certainly no audible thanks. The position of her head shifted very slightly. The doctor saw that she was now looking hard at Sarah. Her face was quite

12

impassive, it had no expression in it. Impossible to tell what was passing in the woman's mind.

Sarah looked at her watch and uttered an exclamation.

" It's much later than I thought." She got up. " Thank you so much, Dr. Gerard, for standing me coffee. I must write some letters now."

He rose and took her hand.

" We shall meet again, I hope," he said.

" Oh, yes! Perhaps you will come to Petra?"

" I shall certainly try to do so."

Sarah smiled at him and turned away. Her way out of the room led her past the Boynton family.

Dr. Gerard, watching, saw Mrs. Boynton's gaze shift to her son's face. He saw the boy's eyes meet hers. As Sarah passed, Raymond Boynton half turned his head—not towards her, but away from her. . . . It was a slow, unwilling motion and conveyed the idea that old Mrs. Boynton had pulled an invisible string.

Sarah King noticed the avoidance, and was young enough and human enough to be annoyed by it. They had had such a friendly talk together in the swaying corridor of the Wagon Lits. They had compared notes on Egypt, had laughed at the ridiculous language of the donkey boys and street touts. Sarah had described how a camel man when he had started hopefully and impudently, " You English lady or American?" had received the answer: " No, Chinese." And her pleasure in seeing the man's complete bewilderment as he stared at her. The boy had been, she thought, like a nice eager schoolboy—there had been, perhaps, something almost pathetic about his eagerness. And now, for no reason at all, he was shy, boorish—positively rude.

" I shan't take any more trouble with him," said Sarah indignantly.

For Sarah, without being unduly conceited, had a fairly good opinion of herself. She knew herself to be definitely attractive to the opposite sex, and she was not one to take a snubbing lying down!

She had been, perhaps, a shade over-friendly to this boy because, for some obscure reason, she had felt sorry for him.

But now, it was apparent, he was merely a rude, stuck-up, boorish young American!

Instead of writing the letters she had mentioned, Sarah King sat down in front of her dressing-table, combed the hair

13

back from her forehead, looked into a pair of troubled hazel eyes in the glass, and took stock of her situation in life.

She had just passed through a difficult emotional crisis. A month ago she had broken off her engagement to a young doctor some four years her senior. They had been very much attracted to each other, but had been too much alike in temperament. Disagreements and quarrels had been of common occurrence. Sarah was of too imperious a temperament herself to brook a calm assertion of autocracy. Like many high-spirited women, Sarah believed herself to admire strength. She had always told herself that she wanted to be mastered. When she met a man capable of mastering her she found that she did not like it at all! To break off her engagement had cost her a good deal of heart-burning, but she was clear-sighted enough to realise that mere mutual attraction was not a sufficient basis on which to build a lifetime of happiness. She had treated herself deliberately to an interesting holiday abroad in order to help on forgetfulness before she went back to start working in earnest.

Sarah's thoughts came back from the past to the present.

" I wonder," she thought, " if Dr. Gerard will let me talk to him about his work. He's done such marvellous work. If only he'll take me seriously. . . . Perhaps—if he comes to Petra——"

Then she thought again of the strange boorish young American.

She had no doubt that it was the presence of his family which had caused him to react in such a peculiar manner, but she felt slightly scornful of him, nevertheless. To be under the thumb of one's family like that—it was really rather ridiculous—especially for a *man*!

And yet. . . .

A queer feeling passed over her. Surely there was something a little *odd* about it all?

She said suddenly out loud: " That boy wants rescuing! I'm going to see to it!"

Chapter 3

WHEN Sarah had left the lounge, Dr. Gerard sat where he was for some minutes. Then he strolled to the table, picked up the latest number of *Le Matin* and strolled with it to a chair a few yards away from the Boynton family. His curiosity was aroused.

He had at first been amused by the English girl's interest in this American family, shrewdly diagnosing that it was inspired by interest in one particular member of the family. But now something out of the ordinary about this family party awakened in him the deeper, more impartial interest of the scientist. He sensed that there was something here of definite psychological interest.

Very discreetly, under the cover of his paper, he took stock of them. First the boy in whom that attractive English girl took such a decided interest. Yes, thought Gerard, definitely the type to appeal to her temperamentally. Sarah King had strength—she possessed well-balanced nerves, cool wits and a resolute will. Dr. Gerard judged the young man to be sensitive, perceptive, diffident and intensely suggestible. He noted with a physician's eye the obvious fact that the boy was at the moment in a state of high nervous tension. Dr. Gerard wondered why. He was puzzled. Why should a young man whose physical health was obviously good, who was abroad ostensibly enjoying himself, be in such a condition that nervous breakdown was imminent?

The doctor turned his attention to the other members of the party. The girl with the chestnut hair was obviously Raymond's sister. They were of the same racial type, small-boned, well-shaped, aristocratic looking. They had the same slender well-formed hands, the same clean line of jaw, and the same poise of the head on a long, slender neck. And the girl, too, was nervous. . . . She made slight involuntary nervous movements, her eyes were deeply shadowed underneath and over bright. Her voice, when she spoke, was too quick and a shade breathless. She was watchful—alert—unable to relax.

" And she is afraid, too," decided Dr. Gerard. " Yes, she is afraid!"

He overheard scraps of conversation—a very ordinary normal conversation.

" We might go to Solomon's Stables?" " Would that be too much for Mother?" " The Wailing Wall in the morning?" " The Temple, of course—the Mosque of Omar they call it—I wonder why?" " Because it's been made into a Moslem mosque, of course, Lennox."

Ordinary commonplace tourists' talk. And yet, somehow, Dr. Gerard felt a queer conviction that these overheard scraps of dialogue were all singularly unreal. They were a mask—a cover for something that surged and eddied underneath—something too deep and formless for words. . . . Again he shot a covert glance from behind the shelter of *Le Matin*.

Lennox? That was the elder brother. The same family likeness could be traced, but there was a difference. Lennox was not so highly strung; he was, Gerard decided, of a less nervous temperament. But about him, too, there seemed something odd. There was no sign of muscular tension about him as there was about the other two. He sat relaxed, limp. Puzzling, searching among memories of patients he had seen sitting like that in hospital wards, Gerard thought:

" He is *exhausted*—yes, exhausted with suffering. That look in the eyes—the look you see in a wounded dog or a sick horse—dumb bestial endurance. . . . It is odd, that. . . . Physically there seems nothing wrong with him. . . . Yet there is no doubt that lately he has been through much suffering—mental suffering—now he no longer suffers—he endures dumbly—waiting, I think, for the blow to fall. . . . What blow? Am I fancying all this? No, the man is waiting for something, for the end to come. So cancer patients lie and wait, thankful that an anodyne dulls the pain a little. . . ."

Lennox Boynton got up and retrieved a ball of wool that the old lady had dropped.

" Here you are, Mother."

" Thank you."

What was she knitting, this monumental impassive old woman? Something thick and coarse. Gerard thought: " Mittens for inhabitants of a workhouse!" And smiled at his own fantasy.

He turned his attention to the youngest member of the party—the girl with the golden red hair. She was, perhaps, nineteen. Her skin had the exquisite clearness that often goes with red hair. Although over thin, it was a beautiful face. She was sitting smiling to herself—smiling into space. There was something a little curious about that smile. It was so far removed from the Solomon Hotel, from Jerusalem. . . . It reminded Dr. Gerard of something. . . . Presently it came to him in a flash. It was the strange unearthly smile that lifts the lips of the Maidens in the Acropolis at Athens—something

16

remote and lovely and a little inhuman. . . . The magic of the smile, her exquisite stillness gave him a little pang.

And then with a shock, Dr. Gerard noticed her hands. They were concealed from the group round her by the table, but he could see them clearly from where he sat. In the shelter of her lap they were picking—picking—tearing a delicate handkerchief into tiny shreds.

It gave him a horrible shock. The aloof remote smile—the still body—and the busy destructive hands. . . .

Chapter 4

There was a slow asthmatic wheezing cough—then the monumental knitting woman spoke.

" Ginevra, you're tired, you'd better go to bed."

The girl started, her fingers stopped their mechanical action. " I'm not tired, Mother."

Gerard recognised appreciatively the musical quality of her voice. It had the sweet singing quality that lends enchantment to the most commonplace utterances.

" Yes, you are. I always know. I don't think you'll be able to do any sightseeing to-morrow."

" Oh! but I shall. I'm quite all right."

In a thick hoarse voice—almost a grating voice, her mother said: " No, you're not. You're going to be ill."

" I'm not! I'm not!"

The girl began trembling violently.

A soft, calm voice said: " I'll come up with you, Jinny."

The quiet young woman with wide, thoughtful grey eyes and neatly-coiled dark hair rose to her feet.

Old Mrs. Boynton said: " No. Let her go up alone."

The girl cried: " I want Nadine to come!"

" Then of course I will." The young woman moved a step forward.

The old woman said: " The child prefers to go by herself— don't you, Jinny?"

There was a pause—a pause of a moment, then Ginevra Boynton said, her voice suddenly flat and dull:

" Yes; I'd rather go alone. Thank you, Nadine."

She moved away, a tall angular figure that moved with a surprising grace.

17

Dr. Gerard lowered his paper and took a full satisfying gaze at old Mrs. Boynton. She was looking after her daughter and her fat face was creased into a peculiar smile. It was, very faintly, a caricature of the lovely unearthly smile that had transformed the girl's face so short a time before.

Then the old woman transferred her gaze to Nadine. The latter had just sat down again. She raised her eyes and met her mother-in-law's glance. Her face was quite imperturbable. The old woman's glance was malicious.

Dr. Gerard thought: " What an absurdity of an old tyrant!"

And then, suddenly, the old woman's eyes were full on him, and he drew in his breath sharply. Small black smouldering eyes they were, but something came from them, a power, a definite force, a wave of evil malignancy. Dr. Gerard knew something about the power of personality. He realised that there was no spoilt tyrannical invalid indulging petty whims. This old woman was a definite force. In the malignancy of her glare he felt a resemblance to the effect produced by a cobra. Mrs. Boynton might be old, infirm, a prey to disease, but she was not powerless. She was a woman who knew the meaning of power, who had exercised a lifetime of power and who had never once doubted her own force. Dr. Gerard had once met a woman who performed a most dangerous and spectacular act with tigers. The great slinking brutes had crawled to their places and performed their degrading and humiliating tricks. Their eyes and subdued snarls told of hatred, bitter fanatical hatred, but they had obeyed, cringed. That had been a young woman, a woman with an arrogant dark beauty, but the look had been the same.

" Une dompteuse," said Dr. Gerard to himself.

And he understood now what that undercurrent to the harmless family talk had been. It was hatred—a dark eddying stream of hatred.

He thought: " How fanciful and absurd most people would think me! Here is a commonplace devoted American family revelling in Palestine—and I weave a story of black magic round it!"

Then he looked with interest at the quiet young woman who was called Nadine. There was a wedding ring on her left hand, and as he watched her he saw her give one swift be-traying glance at the fair-haired, loose-limbed Lennox. He knew, then. . . .

They were man and wife, those two. But it was a mother's glance rather than a wife's—a true mother's glance—protecting, anxious. And he knew something more. He knew that, alone out of that group, Nadine Boynton was unaffected by her mother-in-law's spell. She may have disliked the old woman, but she was not afraid of her. The power did not touch her.

She was unhappy, deeply concerned about her husband, but she was free.

Dr. Gerard said to himself: "All this is very interesting."

Chapter 5

INTO THESE dark imaginings a breath of the commonplace came with almost ludicrous effect.

A man came into the lounge, caught sight of the Boyntons and came across to them. He was a pleasant middle-aged American of a strictly conventional type. He was carefully dressed, with a long clean-shaven face and he had a slow, pleasant, somewhat monotonous voice.

"I was looking around for you all," he said.

Meticulously he shook hands with the entire family. "And how do you find yourself, Mrs. Boynton? Not too tired by the journey?"

Almost graciously, the old lady wheezed out: "No, thank you. My health's never good, as you know——"

"Why, of course, too bad—too bad."

"But I'm certainly no worse."

Mrs. Boynton added with a slow reptilian smile: "Nadine, here, takes good care of me, don't you, Nadine?"

"I do my best." Her voice was expressionless.

"Why, I bet you do," said the stranger heartily. "Well, Lennox, and what do you think of King David's city?"

"Oh, I don't know."

Lennox spoke apathetically—without interest.

"Find it kind of disappointing, do you? I'll confess it struck me that way at first. But perhaps you haven't been around much yet?"

Carol Boynton said: "We can't do very much because of mother."

19

Mrs. Boynton explained: "A couple of hours' sightseeing is about all I can manage every day."

The stranger said heartily: "I think it's wonderful you manage to do all you do, Mrs. Boynton."

Mrs. Boynton gave a slow, wheezy chuckle; it had an almost gloating sound.

"I don't give in to my body! It's the mind that matters! Yes, it's the *mind* . . ."

Her voice died away. Gerard saw Raymond Boynton give a nervous jerk.

"Have you been to the Wailing Wall yet, Mr. Cope?" he asked.

"Why, yes, that was one of the first places I visited. I hope to have done Jerusalem thoroughly in a couple more days, and I'm letting them get me out an itinerary at Cook's so as to do the Holy Land thoroughly—Bethlehem, Nazareth, Tiberias, the Sea of Galilee. It's all going to be mighty interesting. Then there's Jerash, there are some very interesting ruins there —Roman, you know. And I'd very much like to have a look at the Rose Red City of Petra, a most remarkable natural phenomenon, I believe that is—and right off the beaten track— but it takes the best part of a week to get there and back, and do it properly."

Carol said: "I'd love to go there. It sounds marvellous."

"Why, I should say it was definitely worth seeing—yes, definitely worth seeing." Mr. Cope paused, shot a somewhat dubious glance at Mrs. Boynton, and then went on in a voice that to the listening Frenchman was palpably uncertain:

"I wonder now if I couldn't persuade some of you people to come with me? Naturally I know *you* couldn't manage it, Mrs. Boynton, and naturally some of your family would want to remain with you, but if you were to divide forces, so to speak——"

He paused. Gerard heard the even click of Mrs. Boynton's knitting needles. Then she said:

"I don't think we'd care to divide up. We're a very homey group." She looked up. "Well, children, what do you say?"

There was a queer ring in her voice. The answers came promptly. "No, Mother." "Oh, no." "No, of course not."

Mrs. Boynton said, smiling that very odd smile of hers: "You see—they won't leave me. What about you, Nadine? You didn't say anything."

"No, thank you, Mother, not unless Lennox cares about it."

Mrs. Boynton turned her head slowly towards her son.

"Well, Lennox, what about it, why don't you and Nadine go? She seems to want to."

He started—looked up. "I—well—no, I—I think we'd better all stay together."

Mr. Cope said genially: "Well, you *are* a devoted family!" But something in his geniality rang a little hollow and forced.

"We keep to ourselves," said Mrs. Boynton. She began to wind up her ball of wool. "By the way, Raymond, who was that young woman who spoke to you just now?"

Raymond started nervously. He flushed, then went white.

"I—I don't know her name. She—she was on the train the other night."

Mrs. Boynton began slowly to try to heave herself out of her chair.

"I don't think we'll have much to do with her," she said.

Nadine rose and assisted the old woman to struggle out of her chair. She did it with a professional deftness that attracted Gerard's attention.

"Bedtime," said Mrs. Boynton. "Good night, Mr. Cope."

"Good night, Mrs. Boynton. Good night, Mrs. Lennox."

They went off—a little procession. It did not seem to occur to any of the younger members of the party to stay behind.

Mr. Cope was left looking after them. The expression on his face was an odd one.

As Dr. Gerard knew by experience, Americans are disposed to be a friendly race. They have not the uneasy suspicion of the travelling Briton. To a man of Dr. Gerard's tact making the acquaintance of Mr. Cope presented few difficulties. The American was lonely and was, like most of his race, disposed to friendliness. Dr. Gerard's card-case was again to the fore.

Reading the name on it, Mr. Jefferson Cope was duly impressed.

"Why, surely, Dr. Gerard, you were over in the States not very long ago?"

"Last autumn. I was lecturing at Harvard."

"Of course. Yours, Dr. Gerard, is one of the most distinguished names in your profession. You're pretty well at the head of your subject in Paris."

"My dear sir, you are far too kind! I protest."

" No, no, this is a great privilege—meeting you like this. As a matter of fact, there are several very distinguished people here in Jerusalem just at present. There's yourself and there's Lord Welldon, and Sir Gabriel Steinbaum, the financier. Then there's the veteran English archæologist, Sir Manders Stone. And there's Lady Westholme, who's very prominent in English politics. And there's that famous Belgian detective, Hercule Poirot."

" Little Hercule Poirot? Is he here?"

" I read his name in the local paper as having lately arrived. Seems to me all the world and his wife are at the Solomon Hotel. A mighty fine hotel it is, too. And very tastefully decorated."

Mr. Jefferson Cope was clearly enjoying himself. Dr. Gerard was a man who could display a lot of charm when he chose. Before long the two men had adjourned to the bar.

After a couple of highballs Gerard said: " Tell me, is that a typical American family to whom you were talking?"

Jefferson Cope sipped his drink thoughtfully. Then he said: " Why, no, I wouldn't say it was exactly typical."

" No? A very devoted family, I thought."

Mr. Cope said slowly: " You mean they all seem to revolve round the old lady? That's true enough. She's a very remarkable old lady, you know."

" Indeed?"

Mr. Cope needed very little encouragement. The gentle invitation was enough.

" I don't mind telling you, Dr. Gerard, I've been having that family a good deal on my mind lately. I've been thinking about them a lot. If I may say so, it would ease my mind to talk to you about the matter. If it won't bore you, that is?"

Dr. Gerard disclaimed boredom. Mr. Jefferson Cope went on slowly, his pleasant clean-shaven face creased with perplexity.

" I'll tell you straight away that I'm just a little worried. Mrs. Boynton, you see, is an old friend of mine. That is to say, not the old Mrs. Boynton, the young one, Mrs. Lennox Boynton."

" Ah, yes, that very charming dark-haired young lady."

" That's right. That's Nadine. Nadine Boynton, Dr. Gerard, is a very lovely character. I knew her before she was married. She was in hospital then, working to be a trained nurse. Then

22

she went for a vacation to stay with the Boyntons and she married Lennox."

" Yes?"

Mr. Jefferson Cope took another sip of highball and went on:

" I'd like to tell you, Dr. Gerard, just a little of the Boynton family history."

" Yes? I should be most interested."

" Well, you see, the late Elmer Boynton—he was quite a well-known man and a very charming personality—was twice married. His first wife died when Carol and Raymond were tiny toddlers. The second Mrs. Boynton, so I've been told, was a handsome woman when he married her, though not very young. Seems odd to think she can ever have been handsome to look at her now, but that's what I've been told on very good authority. Anyway, her husband thought a lot of her and adopted her judgment on almost every point. He was an invalid for some years before he died, and she practically ruled the roost. She's a very capable woman with a fine head for business. A very conscientious woman, too. After Elmer died, she devoted herself absolutely to these children. There's one of her own, too, Ginevra—pretty red-haired girl, but a bit delicate. Well, as I was telling you, Mrs. Boynton devoted herself entirely to her family. She just shut out the outside world entirely. Now I don't know what you think, Dr. Gerard, but I don't think that's always a very sound thing."

" I agree with you. It is most harmful to developing mentalities."

" Yes, I should say that just about expresses it. Mrs. Boynton shielded these children from the outside world and never let them make any outside contacts. The result of that is that they've grown up—well, kind of nervy. They're jumpy, if you know what I mean. Can't make friends with strangers. It's bad, that."

" It is very bad."

" I've no doubt Mrs. Boynton meant well. It was just over-devotion on her part."

" They all live at home?" asked the doctor.

" Yes."

" Do neither of the sons work?"

" Why, no. Elmer Boynton was a rich man. He left all his money to Mrs. Boynton for her lifetime—but it was understood that it was for the family upkeep generally."

23

" So they are dependent on her financially?"

" That is so. And she's encouraged them to live at home and not go out and look for jobs. Well, maybe that's all right, there's plenty of money, they don't need to take a job, but I think for the male sex, anyway, work's a good tonic. Then, there's another thing—they've none of them got any hobbies. They don't play golf. They don't belong to any country club. They don't go around to dances or do anything with the other young people. They live in a great barrack of a house way down in the country miles from anywhere. I tell you, Dr. Gerard, it seems all wrong to me."

" I agree with you," said Dr. Gerard.

" Not one of them has got the least social sense. The community spirit—that's what's lacking! They may be a very devoted family, but they're all bound up in themselves."

" There has never been any question of one or other of them branching out for him or herself?"

" Not that I've heard of. They just sit around."

" Do you put the blame for that on them or on Mrs. Boynton?"

Jefferson Cope shifted uneasily.

" Well, in a sense, I feel she is more or less responsible. It's bad bringing-up on her part. All the same. when a young fellow comes to maturity it's up to him to kick over the traces of his own accord. No boy ought to keep on being tied to his mother's apron strings. He ought to choose to be independent."

Dr. Gerard said thoughtfully: " That might be impossible."

" Why impossible?"

" There are methods, Mr. Cope, of preventing a tree from growing."

Cope stared. " They're a fine healthy lot, Dr. Gerard."

" The mind can be stunted and warped as well as the body."

" They're bright mentally, too."

Jefferson Cope went on: " No, Dr. Gerard, take it from me, a man has got the control of his own destiny right there in his own hands. A man who respects himself strikes out on his own and makes something of his life. He doesn't just sit round and twiddle his thumbs. No woman ought to respect a man who does that."

Gerard looked at him curiously for a minute or two. Then

he said: "You refer particularly, I think, to Mr. Lennox Boynton?"

"Why, yes, it was Lennox I was thinking of. Raymond's only a boy still. But Lennox is just on thirty. Time he showed he was made of something."

"It is a difficult life, perhaps, for his wife?"

"Of course it's a difficult life for her! Nadine is a very fine girl. I admire her more than I can say. She's never let drop one word of complaint. *But she's not happy*, Dr. Gerard. She's just as unhappy as she can be."

Gerard nodded his head.

"Yes, I think that well might be."

"I don't know what *you* think about it, Dr. Gerard, but *I* think that there's a limit to what a woman ought to put up with! If I were Nadine I'd put it to young Lennox straight. Either he sets to and proves what he's made of, or else——"

"Or else, you think, she should leave him?"

"She's got her own life to live, Dr. Gerard. If Lennox doesn't appreciate her as she ought to be appreciated—well, there are other men who will."

"There is—yourself, for instance?"

The American flushed. Then he looked straight at the other with a certain simple dignity.

"That's so," he said. "I'm not ashamed of my feeling for that lady. I respect her and I am very deeply attached to her. All I want is her happiness. If she were happy with Lennox, I'd sit right back and fade out of the picture."

"But as it is?"

"But as it is I'm standing by! If she wants me, *I'm here!*"

"You are, in fact, the *parfait gentil* knight," murmured Gerard.

"Pardon?"

"My dear sir, chivalry only lives nowadays in the American nation! You are content to serve your lady without hope of reward! It is most admirable, that! What exactly do you hope to be able to do for her?"

"My idea is to be right here at hand if she needs me."

"And what, may I ask, is the older Mrs. Boynton's attitude towards you?"

Jefferson Cope said slowly: "I'm never quite sure about that old lady. As I've told you, she isn't fond of making outside contacts. But she's been different to me, she's always very gracious and treats me quite like one of the family."

"In fact, she approves of your friendship with Mrs. Lennox?"

"She does."

Dr. Gerard shrugged his shoulders.

"That is, perhaps, a little odd?"

Jefferson Cope said stiffly: "Let me assure you, Dr. Gerard, there is nothing dishonourable in that friendship. It is purely platonic."

"My dear sir, I am quite sure of that. I repeat, though, that for Mrs. Boynton to encourage that friendship is a curious action on her part. You know, Mr. Cope, Mrs. Boynton interests me—she interests me greatly."

"She is certainly a remarkable woman. She has great force of character—a most prominent personality. As I say, Elmer Boynton had the greatest faith in her judgment."

"So much so that he was content to leave his children completely at her mercy from the financial point of view. In my country, Mr. Cope, it is impossible by law to do such a thing."

Mr. Cope rose. "In America," he said, "we're great believers in absolute freedom."

Dr. Gerard rose also. He was unimpressed by the remark. He had heard it made before by people of many different nationalities. The illusion that freedom is the prerogative of one's own particular race is fairly widespread.

Dr. Gerard was wiser. He knew that no race, no country and no individual could be described as free. But he also knew that there were different degrees of bondage.

He went up to bed thoughtful and interested.

Chapter 6

SARAH KING stood in the precincts of the Temple—the Haram-esh-Sherif. Her back was to the Dome of the Rock. The splashing of fountains sounded in her ears. Little groups of tourists passed by without disturbing the peace of the oriental atmosphere.

Strange, thought Sarah, that once a Jebusite should have made this rocky summit into a threshing floor and that David should have purchased it for six hundred shekels of gold and made it a Holy Place. And now the loud chattering tongues of sightseers of all nations could be heard.

She turned and looked at the Mosque which now covered the shrine and wondered if Solomon's temple would have looked half as beautiful.

There was a clatter of footsteps and a little party came out from the interior of the Mosque. It was the Boyntons escorted by a voluble dragoman. Mrs. Boynton was supported between Lennox and Raymond. Nadine and Mr. Cope walked behind. Carol came last. As they were moving off, the latter caught sight of Sarah.

She hesitated, then, on a sudden decision, she wheeled round and ran swiftly and noiselessly across the courtyard.

" Excuse me," she said breathlessly. " I must—I—I felt I must speak to you."

" Yes?" said Sarah.

Carol was trembling violently. Her face was quite white.

" It's about—my brother. When you—you spoke to him last night you must have thought him very rude. But he didn't mean to be—he—he couldn't help it. Oh, do please believe me."

Sarah felt that the whole scene was ridiculous. Both her pride and her good taste were offended. Why should a strange girl suddenly rush up and tender a ridiculous apology for a boorish brother?

An off-hand reply trembled on her lips—and then, quickly, her mood changed.

There was something out of the ordinary here. This girl was in deadly earnest. That something in Sarah which had led her to adopt a medical career reacted to the girl's need. Her instinct told her there was something badly wrong.

She said encouragingly: " Tell me about it."

" He spoke to you on the train, didn't he?" began Carol.

Sarah nodded. " Yes; at least, I spoke to him."

" Oh, of course. It would be that way round. But, you see, last night Ray was afraid——"

She stopped.

" Afraid?"

Carol's white face crimsoned.

" Oh, I know it sounds absurd—mad. You, see, my mother —she's—she's not well—and she doesn't like us making friends outside. But—but I know Ray would—would like to be friends with you."

27

Sarah was interested. Before she could speak, Carol went on: " I—I know what I'm saying sounds very silly, but we are —rather an odd family." She cast a quick look round—it was a look of fear.

" I—I mustn't stay," she murmured. " They may miss me."

Sarah made up her mind. She spoke.

" Why shouldn't you stay—if you want to? We might walk back together."

" Oh, no." Carol drew back. " I—I couldn't do that."

" Why not?" said Sarah.

" I couldn't really. My mother would be—would be——"

Sarah said clearly and calmly:

" I know it's awfully difficult sometimes for parents to realise that their children are grown up. They will go on trying to run their lives for them. But it's a pity, you know, to give in! One must stand up for one's rights."

Carol murmured: " You don't understand—you don't understand in the least. . . ."

Her hands twisted together nervously.

Sarah went on: " One gives in sometimes because one is afraid of rows. Rows are very unpleasant, but I think freedom of action is always worth fighting for."

" Freedom?" Carol stared at her. " None of us have ever been free. We never will be."

" Nonsense!" said Sarah clearly.

Carol leaned forward and touched her arm.

" Listen. I *must* try and make you understand! Before her marriage my mother—she's my stepmother really—was a wardress in a prison. My father was the Governor and he married her. Well, *it's been like that ever since*. She's gone on being a wardress—*to us*. That's why our life is just—being in prison!"

Her head jerked round again.

" They've missed me. I—I must go."

Sarah caught her by the arm as she was darting off.

" One minute. We must meet again and talk."

" I can't. I shan't be able to."

" Yes, you can." She spoke authoritatively. " Come to my room after you go to bed. It's 319. Don't forget 319."

She released her hold. Carol ran off after her family.

Sarah stood staring after her. She awoke from her thoughts to find Dr. Gerard by her side.

28

" Good morning, Miss King. So you've been talking to Miss Carol Boynton?"

" Yes, we had the most extraordinary conversation. Let me tell you."

She repeated the substance of her conversation with the girl. Gerard pounced on one point.

" Wardress in a prison, was she, that old hippopotamus? That is significant, perhaps."

Sarah said:

" You mean that that is the cause of her tyranny? It is the habit of her former profession."

Gerard shook his head.

" No, that is approaching it from the wrong angle. There is some deep underlying compulsion. She does not love tyranny *because she has been a wardress*. Let us rather say that *she became a wardress because she loved tyranny*. In my theory it was a secret desire for power over other human beings that led her to adopt that profession."

His face was very grave.

" There are such strange things buried down in the unconscious. A lust for power—a lust for cruelty—a savage desire to tear and rend—all the inheritance of our past racial memories. . . . They are all there, Miss King, all the cruelty and savagery and lust. . . . We shut the door on them and deny them conscious life, but sometimes—they are too strong."

Sarah shivered. " I know."

Gerard continued: " We see it all round us to-day—in political creeds, in the conduct of nations. A reaction from humanitarianism—from pity—from brotherly good-will. The creeds sound well sometimes—a wise régime—a beneficent government—but imposed by *force*—resting on a basis of cruelty and fear. They are opening the door, these apostles of violence, they are letting up the old savagery, the old delight in cruelty *for its own sake*! Oh, it is difficult—Man is an animal very delicately balanced. He has one prime necessity—to survive. To advance too quickly is as fatal as to lag behind. He must survive! He must, perhaps, retain some of the old savagery, but he must not—no definitely he must not—*deify* it!"

There was a pause. Then Sarah said:

" You think old Mrs. Boynton is a kind of Sadist?"

" I am almost sure of it. I think she rejoices in the infliction

29

of pain—mental pain, mind you, not physical. That is very much rarer and very much more difficult to deal with. She likes to have control of other human beings and she likes to make them suffer."

" It's pretty beastly," said Sarah.

Gerard told her of his conversation with Jefferson Cope. " He doesn't realise what is going on?" she said thoughtfully.

" How should he? He is not a psychologist."

" True. He hasn't got our disgusting minds!"

" Exactly. He has a nice upright, sentimental, normal American mind. He believes in good rather than evil. He sees that the atmosphere of the Boynton family is all wrong, but he credits Mrs. Boynton with misguided devotion rather than active maleficence."

" That must amuse her," said Sarah.

" I should imagine it does!"

Sarah said impatiently:

" But why don't they break away? They could."

Gerard shook his head.

" No, there you are wrong. *They cannot*. Have you ever seen the old experiment with a cock? You chalk a line on the floor and put the cock's beak on it. The cock believes he is tied there. He cannot raise his head. So with these unfortunates. She has worked on them, remember, since they were children. And her dominance has been mental. She has hypnotised them to believe that *they cannot disobey her*. Oh, I know most people would say that was nonsense—but you and I know better. She has made them believe that utter dependence on her is inevitable. They have been in prison so long that if the prison door stands open they would no longer notice! One of them, at least, no longer even wants to be free! And they would all be *afraid* of freedom."

Sarah asked practically: " What will happen when she dies?"

Gerard shrugged his shoulders.

" It depends. On how soon that happens. If it happened *now*—well, I think it might not be too late. The boy and girl —they are still young—impressionable. They would become, I believe, normal human beings. With Lennox, possibly, it has gone too far. He looks to me like a man who has parted company with hope—he lives and endures like a brute beast."

30

Sarah said impatiently: "His wife ought to have done something! She ought to have yanked him out of it."

"I wonder. She may have tried—and failed."

"Do you think she's under the spell, too?"

Gerard shook his head.

"No. I don't think the old lady has any power over her, and for that reason she hates her with a bitter hatred. Watch her eyes."

Sarah frowned. "I can't make her out—the young one, I mean. Does she know what is going on?"

"I think she must have a pretty shrewd idea."

"H'm," said Sarah. "That old woman ought to be murdered! Arsenic in her early morning tea would be my prescription."

Then she said abruptly:

"What about the youngest girl—the red-haired one with the rather fascinating vacant smile?"

Gerard frowned. "I don't know. There is something queer there. Ginevra Boynton is the old woman's own daughter, of course."

"Yes. I suppose that would be different—or wouldn't it?"

Gerard said slowly: "I do not believe that when once the mania for power (and the lust for cruelty) has taken possession of a human being it can spare *anybody*—not even its nearest and dearest."

He was silent for a moment, then he said: "Are you a Christian, mademoiselle?"

Sarah said slowly: "I don't know. I used to think that I wasn't anything. But now—I'm not sure. I feel—oh, I feel that if I could sweep all this away"—she made a violent gesture—"all the buildings and the sects and the fierce squabbling churches—that—that I might see Christ's quiet figure riding into Jerusalem on a donkey—and believe in Him."

Dr. Gerard said gravely: "I believe at least in one of the chief tenets of the Christian faith—*contentment with a lowly place*. I am a doctor and I know that ambition—the desire to succeed—to have power—leads to most ills of the human soul. If the desire is realised it leads to arrogance, violence and final satiety—and if it is denied—ah! if it is denied—let all the asylums for the insane rise up and give their testimony! They are filled with human beings who were unable to face being mediocre, insignificant, ineffective and who therefore created

31

for themselves ways of escape from reality so as to be shut off from life itself for ever."

Sarah said abruptly: "It's a pity the old Boynton woman isn't in an asylum."

Gerard shook his head.

"No—her place is not there among the failures. It is worse than that. She has succeeded, you see! She has accomplished her dream."

Sarah shuddered.

She cried passionately: "Such things ought not to be!"

Chapter 7

SARAH WONDERED very much whether Carol Boynton would keep her appointment that night.

On the whole she rather doubted it. She was afraid that Carol would have a sharp reaction after her semi-confidences of the morning.

Nevertheless she made her preparations, slipping on a blue satin dressing-gown and getting out her little spirit lamp and boiling up water.

She was just on the point of giving Carol up (it was after one o'clock) and going to bed, when there was a tap on her door. She opened it and drew quickly back to let Carol come in.

The latter said breathlessly: "I was afraid you might have gone to bed. . . ."

Sarah's manner was carefully matter-of-fact.

"Oh, no, I was waiting for you. Have some tea, will you? It's real Lapsang Souchong."

She brought over a cup. Carol had been nervous and uncertain of herself. Now she accepted the cup and a biscuit and her manner became calmer.

"This is rather fun," said Sarah, smiling.

Carol looked a little startled.

"Yes," she said doubtfully. "Yes, I suppose it is."

"Rather like the midnight feasts we used to have at school," went on Sarah. "I suppose you didn't go to school?"

Carol shook her head.

"No, we never left home. We had a governess—different governesses. They never stayed long."

"Did you never go away at all?"

"No. We've lived always in the same house. This coming abroad is the first time I've ever been away."

Sarah said casually: "It must have been a great adventure."

"Oh, it was. It—it's all been like a dream."

"What made your—your stepmother decide to come abroad?"

At the mention of Mrs. Boynton's name, Carol had flinched. Sarah said quickly:

"You know, I'm by way of being a doctor. I've just taken my M.B. Your mother—or stepmother rather—is very interesting to me—as a case, you know. I should say she was quite definitely a pathological case."

Carol stared. It was clearly a very unexpected point of view to her: Sarah had spoken as she had with deliberate intent. She realised that to her family Mrs. Boynton loomed as a kind of powerful obscene idol. It was Sarah's object to rob her of her more terrifying aspect.

"Yes," she said. "There's a kind of disease of—of grandeur—that gets hold of people. They get very autocratic and insist on everything being done exactly as they say and are altogether very difficult to deal with."

Carol put down her cup.

"Oh," she cried, "I'm so glad to be talking to you. Really, you know, I believe Ray and I have been getting quite—well, quite queer. We'd get terribly worked up about things."

"Talking with an outsider is always a good thing," said Sarah. "Inside a family one is apt to get too intense." Then she asked casually: "If you are unhappy, haven't you ever thought of leaving home?"

Carol looked startled. "Oh, no! How could we? I—I mean mother would never allow it."

"But she couldn't stop you," said Sarah gently. "You're over age."

"I'm twenty-three."

"Exactly."

"But still, I don't see how—I mean, I wouldn't know where to go and what to do."

Her tone seemed bewildered.

"You see," she said, "we haven't got any money."

"Haven't you any friends you could go to?"

"Friends?" Carol shook her head. "Oh, no, we don't know anyone!"

" Did none of you ever think of leaving home?"

" No—I don't think so. Oh—oh—we couldn't."

Sarah changed the subject. She found the girl's bewilderment pitiful.

She said: " Are you fond of your stepmother?"

Slowly Carol shook her head. She whispered in a low scared voice: " I hate her. So does Ray. . . . We've—we've often wished she would die."

Again Sarah changed the subject.

" Tell me about your elder brother."

" Lennox? I don't know what's the matter with Lennox. He hardly ever speaks now. He goes about in a kind of daydream. Nadine's terribly worried about him."

" You are fond of your sister-in-law?"

" Yes, Nadine is different. She's always kind. But she's very unhappy."

" About your brother?"

" Yes."

" Have they been married long?"

" Four years."

" And they've always lived at home?"

" Yes."

Sarah asked: " Does your sister-in-law like that?"

" No."

There was a pause. Then Carol said:

" There was an awful fuss just over four years ago. You see, as I told you, none of us ever go outside the house at home. I mean we go into the grounds, but nowhere else. But Lennox did. He got out at night. He went into Fountain Springs—there was a sort of dance going on. Mother was frightfully angry when she found out. It was terrible. And then, after that, she asked Nadine to come and stay. Nadine was a very distant cousin of father's. She was very poor and was training to be a hospital nurse. She came and stayed with us for a month. I can't tell you how exciting it was to have someone to stay! And she and Lennox fell in love with each other. And mother said they'd better be married quickly and live on with us."

" And was Nadine willing to do that?"

Carol hesitated.

" I don't think she wanted to do that very much, but she didn't really *mind*. Then, later, she wanted to go away—with Lennox, of course——"

34

"But they didn't go?" asked Sarah.

"No, mother wouldn't hear of it."

Carol paused, and then said:

"I don't think—she likes Nadine any longer. Nadine is—funny. You never know what she's thinking. She tries to help Jinny and mother doesn't like it."

"Jinny is your youngest sister?"

"Yes. Ginevra is her real name."

"Is she—unhappy, too?"

Carol shook her head doubtfully.

"Jinny's been very queer lately. I don't understand her. You see, she's always been rather delicate—and—and mother fusses about her and—and it makes her worse. And lately Jinny has been very queer indeed. She—she frightens me sometimes. She—she doesn't always know what she's doing."

"Has she seen a doctor?"

"No, Nadine wanted her to, but mother said no—and Jinny got very hysterical and screamed, and said she wouldn't see a doctor. But I'm worried about her."

Suddenly Carol rose.

"I musn't keep you up. It's—it's very good of you letting me come and talk to you. You must think us very odd as a family."

"Oh, everybody's odd, really," said Sarah lightly. "Come again, will you? And bring your brother, if you like."

"May I really?"

"Yes; we'll do some secret plotting. I'd like you to meet a friend of mine, too, a Dr. Gerard, an awfully nice Frenchman."

The colour came into Carol's cheeks.

"Oh, what fun it sounds. If only mother doesn't find out!"

Sarah suppressed her original retort and said instead, "Why should she? Good night. Shall we say to-morrow night at the same time?"

"Oh, yes. The day after, you see, we may be going away."

"Then let's have a definite date for to-morrow. Good night."

"Good night—and thank you."

Carol went out of the room and slipped noiselessly along the corridor. Her own room was on the floor above. She reached it, opened the door—and stood appalled on the threshold.

Mrs. Boynton was sitting in an arm-chair by the fireplace in a crimson wool dressing-gown.

A little cry escaped from Carol's lips. " Oh! "

A pair of black eyes bored into hers.

" Where have you been, Carol? "

" I—I—— "

" Where have you been? "

A soft, husky voice with that queer menacing undertone in it that always made Carol's heart beat with unreasoning terror.

" To see a Miss King—Sarah King. "

" The girl who spoke to Raymond the other evening? "

" Yes, Mother. "

" Have you made any plans to see her again? "

Carol's lips moved soundlessly. She nodded assent. Fright—great sickening waves of fright. . . .

" When? "

" To-morrow night. "

" You are not to go. You understand? "

" Yes, Mother. "

" You promise? "

" Yes—yes. "

Mrs. Boynton struggled to get up. Mechanically Carol came forward and helped her. Mrs. Boynton walked slowly across the room, supporting herself on her stick. She paused in the doorway and looked back at the cowering girl.

" You are to have nothing more to do with this Miss King. You understand? "

" Yes, Mother. "

" Repeat it. "

" I am to have nothing more to do with her. "

" Good. "

Mrs. Boynton went out and shut the door.

Stiffly, Carol moved across the bedroom. She felt sick, her whole body felt wooden and unreal. She dropped on to the bed and suddenly she was shaken by a storm of weeping.

It was as though a vista had opened before her—a vista of sunlight and trees and flowers. . . .

Now the black walls had closed round her once more.

Chapter 8

" CAN I speak to you a minute?"

Nadine Boynton turned in surprise, staring into the dark eager face of an entirely unknown young woman.

" Why, certainly."

But as she spoke, almost unconsciously she threw a quick, nervous glance over her shoulder.

" My name is Sarah King," went on the other.

" Oh, yes?"

" Mrs. Boynton, I'm going to say something rather odd to you. I talked to your sister-in-law for quite a long time the other evening."

A faint shadow seemed to ruffle the serenity of Nadine Boynton's face.

" You talked to Ginevra?"

" No, not to Ginevra—to Carol."

The shadow lifted.

" Oh, I see—to Carol."

Nadine Boynton seemed pleased, but very much surprised. " How did you manage that?"

Sarah said: " She came to my room—quite late."

She saw the faint raising of the pencilled brows on the white forehead. She said with some embarrassment: " I'm sure this must seem very odd to you."

" No," said Nadine Boynton. " I am very glad. Very glad indeed. It is very nice for Carol to have a friend to talk to."

" We—we got on very well together." Sarah tried to choose her words carefully. " In fact we arranged to—to meet again the following night."

" Yes."

" But Carol didn't come."

" Didn't she?"

Nadine's voice was cool—reflective. Her face, so quiet and gentle, told Sarah nothing.

" No. Yesterday she was passing through the hall. I spoke to her and she didn't answer. Just looked at me once, and then away again, and hurried on."

" I see."

There was a pause. Sarah found it difficult to go on. Nadine Boynton said presently: " I'm—very sorry. Carol is—rather a nervous girl."

Again that pause. Sarah took her courage in both hands. " You know, Mrs. Boynton, I'm by way of being a doctor. I think—I think it would be good for your sister-in-law not to —not to shut herself away too much from people."

Nadine Boynton looked thoughtfully at Sarah.

She said: " I see. You're a doctor. That makes a difference."

" You see what I mean?" Sarah urged.

Nadine bent her head. She was still thoughtful.

" You are quite right, of course," she said after a minute or two. " But there are difficulties. My mother-in-law is in bad health and she has what I can only describe as a morbid dislike of any outsiders penetrating into her family circle."

Sarah said mutinously: " But Carol is a grown-up woman."

Nadine Boynton shook her head.

" Oh, no," she said. " In body, but not in mind. If you talked to her you must have noticed that. In an emergency she would always behave like a frightened child."

" Do you think that's what happened? Do you think she became—afraid?"

" I should imagine, Miss King, that my mother-in-law insisted on Carol having nothing more to do with you."

" And Carol gave in?"

Nadine Boynton said quietly: " Can you really imagine her doing anything else?"

The eyes of the two women met. Sarah felt that behind the mask of conventional words they understood each other. Nadine, she felt, understood the position. But she was clearly not prepared to discuss it in any way.

Sarah felt discouraged. The other evening it had seemed to her as though half the battle were won. By means of secret meetings she would imbue Carol with the spirit of revolt—yes, and Raymond, too. (Be honest now, wasn't it Raymond really she had had in mind all along?) And now, in the very first round of the battle she had been ignominiously defeated by that hulk of shapeless flesh with her evil, gloating eyes. Carol had capitulated without a struggle.

" It's all *wrong*!" cried Sarah.

Nadine did not answer. Something in her silence went home to Sarah like a cold hand laid on her heart. She thought:

"This woman knows the hopelessness of it much better than I do. She's *lived* with it!"

The lift gates opened. The older Mrs. Boynton emerged. She leaned on a stick and Raymond supported her on the other side.

Sarah gave a slight start. She saw the old woman's eyes sweep from her to Nadine and back again. She had been prepared for dislike in those eyes—for hatred even. She was not prepared for what she saw—a triumphant and malicious enjoyment. Sarah turned away. Nadine went forward and joined the other two.

"So there you are, Nadine," said Mrs. Boynton. "I'll sit down and rest a little before I go out."

They settled her in a high-backed chair. Nadine sat down beside her.

"Who were you talking to, Nadine?"

"A Miss King."

"Oh, yes. The girl who spoke to Raymond the other night. Well, Ray, why don't you go and speak to her now? She's over there at the writing-table."

The old woman's mouth widened into a malicious smile as she looked at Raymond. His face flushed. He turned his head away and muttered something.

"What's that you say, son?"

"I don't want to speak to her."

"No, I thought not. You won't speak to her. You couldn't, however much you wanted to!"

She coughed suddenly—a wheezing cough.

"I'm enjoying this trip, Nadine," she said. "I wouldn't have missed it for anything."

"No?"

Nadine's voice was expressionless.

"Ray."

"Yes, Mother?"

"Get me a piece of notepaper—from the table over there in the corner."

Raymond went off obediently. Nadine raised her head. She watched, not the boy, but the old woman. Mrs. Boynton was leaning forward, her nostrils dilated as though with pleasure. Ray passed close by Sarah. She looked up, a sudden hope showing in her face. It died down as he brushed past her, took some notepaper from the case and went back across the room.

There were little beads of sweat on his forehead as he rejoined them, and his face was dead white.

Very softly Mrs. Boynton murmured: "Ah . . ." as she watched his face.

Then she saw Nadine's eyes fixed on her. Something in them made her own snap with sudden anger.

"Where's Mr. Cope this morning?" she said.

Nadine's eyes dropped again. She answered in her gentle, expressionless voice:

"I don't know. I haven't seen him."

"I like him," said Mrs. Boynton. "I like him very much. We must see a good deal of him. You'll like that, won't you?"

"Yes," said Nadine. "I, too, like him very much."

"What's the matter with Lennox lately? He seems very dull and quiet. Nothing wrong between you, is there?"

"Oh, no. Why should there be?"

"I wondered. Married people don't always hit it off. Perhaps you'd be happier living in a home of your own?"

Nadine did not answer.

"Well, what do you say to the idea? Does it appeal to you?"

Nadine shook her head. She said, smiling: "I don't think it would appeal to *you*, Mother."

Mrs. Boynton's eyelids flickered. She said sharply and venomously: "You've always been against me, Nadine."

The younger woman replied evenly:

"I'm sorry you should think that."

The old woman's hand closed on her stick. Her face seemed to get a shade more purple.

She said, with a change of tone: "I forgot my drops. Get them for me, Nadine."

"Certainly."

Nadine got up and crossed the lounge to the lift. Mrs. Boynton looked after her. Raymond sat limply in a chair, his eyes glazed with dull misery.

Nadine went upstairs and along the corridor. She entered the sitting-room of their suite. Lennox was sitting by the window. There was a book in his hand, but he was not reading. He roused himself as Nadine came in. "Hallo, Nadine."

"I've come up for mother's drops. She forgot them."

She went on into Mrs. Boynton's bedroom. From a bottle

on the washstand she carefully measured a dose into a small medicine glass, filling it up with water. As she passed through the sitting-room again she paused.

"Lennox."

It was a moment or two before he answered her. It was as though the message had a long way to travel.

Then he said: "I beg your pardon. What is it?"

Nadine Boynton set down the glass carefully on the table. Then she went over and stood beside him.

"Lennox, look at the sunshine—out there, through the window. Look at life. It's beautiful. We might be out in it—instead of being here looking through a window."

Again there was a pause. Then he said: "I'm sorry. Do you want to go out?"

She answered him quickly: "Yes, I want to go out—*with you*—out into the sunshine—out into life—and live—the two of us together."

He shrank back into his chair. His eyes looked restless, hunted.

"Nadine, my dear—must we go into all this again?"

"Yes, we must. Let us go away and lead our own life somewhere."

"How can we? We've no money."

"We can earn money."

"How could we? What could we do? I'm untrained. Thousands of men—qualified men—trained men—are out of a job as it is. We couldn't manage it."

"I would earn money for both of us."

"My dear child, you'd never even completed your training. It's hopeless—impossible."

"No, what is hopeless and impossible is our present life."

"You don't know what you are talking about. Mother is very good to us. She gives us every luxury."

"Except freedom. Lennox, make an effort. Come with me now—to-day——"

"Nadine, I think you're quite mad."

"No, I'm sane. Absolutely and completely sane. I want a life of my own, with you, in the sunshine—not stifled in the shadow of an old woman who is a tyrant and who delights in making you unhappy."

"Mother may be rather an autocrat——"

"Your mother is mad! She's insane!"

He answered mildly: " That's not true. She's got a remarkably good head for business."

" Perhaps—yes."

" And you must realise, Nadine, she can't live for ever. She's getting old and she's in very bad health. At her death my father's money is divided equally among us share and share alike. You remember, she read us the will?"

" When she dies," said Nadine. " It may be too late."

" Too late?"

" Too late for happiness."

Lennox murmured: " Too late for happiness." He shivered suddenly. Nadine went closer to him. She put her hand on his shoulder.

" Lennox, I love you. It's a battle between me and your mother. Are you going to be on her side or mine?"

" On yours—on yours!"

" Then do what I ask."

" It's impossible!"

" No, it's not impossible. Think, Lennox, we could have children. . . ."

" Mother wants us to have children. She has said so."

" I know, but I won't bring children into the world to live in the shadow you have all been brought up in. Your mother can influence you, but she's no power over me."

Lennox murmured: " You make her angry sometimes, Nadine; it isn't wise."

" She is only angry because she knows that she can't influence my mind or dictate my thoughts!"

" I know you are always polite and gentle with her. You're wonderful. You're too good for me. You always have been. When you said you would marry me it was like an unbelievable dream."

Nadine said quietly: " I was wrong to marry you."

Lennox said hopelessly: " Yes, you were wrong."

" You don't understand. What I mean is that if I had gone away then and asked you to follow me you would have done so. Yes, I really believe you would. . . . I was not clever enough then to understand your mother and what she wanted."

She paused, then she said: " You refuse to come away? Well, I can't make you. But *I* am free to go! I think—I think I *shall* go. . . ."

He stared up at her incredulously. For the first time his

reply came quickly, as though at last the sluggish current of his thoughts was accelerated. He stammered: " But—but—you can't do that. Mother—mother would never hear of it."

" She couldn't stop me."

" You've no money."

" I could make, borrow, beg or steal it. Understand, Lennox, your mother has no power over me! I can go or stay at my will. I am beginning to feel that I have borne this life long enough."

" Nadine—don't leave me—don't leave me. . . ."

She looked at him thoughtfully—quietly—with an inscrutable expression.

" Don't leave me, Nadine."

He spoke like a child. She turned her head away, so that he should not see the sudden pain in her eyes.

She knelt down beside him.

" *Then come with me.* Come with me! You can. Indeed you can if you only will!"

He shrank back from her.

" I can't. I can't. I tell you. I haven't—God help me—*I haven't the courage. . . .*"

Chapter 9

DR. GERARD walked into the office of Messrs. Castle, the tourist agents, and found Sarah King at the counter.

She looked up.

" Oh, good morning. I'm fixing up my tour to Petra. I've just heard you are going after all."

" Yes, I find I can just manage it."

" How nice."

" Shall we be a large party, I wonder?"

" They say just two other women—and you and me. One car load."

" That will be delightful," said Gerard, with a little bow. Then he, in turn, attended to his business.

Presently, holding his mail in his hands, he joined Sarah as she stepped out of the office. It was a crisp, sunny day, with a slight cold tang in the air.

" What news of our friends, the Boyntons?" asked Dr.

Gerard. "I have been to Bethlehem and Nazareth and other places—a tour of three days."

Slowly and rather unwillingly, Sarah narrated her abortive efforts to establish contact.

"Anyhow, I failed," she finished. "And they're leaving to-day."

"Where are they going?"

"I've no idea."

She went on vexedly: "I feel, you know, that I've made rather a fool of myself!"

"In what way?"

"Interfering in other people's business."

Gerard shrugged his shoulders.

"That is a matter of opinion."

"You mean whether one should interfere or not?"

"Yes."

"Do you?"

The Frenchman looked amused.

"You mean, is it my habit to concern myself with other people's affairs? I will say to you frankly: No."

"Then you think I'm wrong to have tried butting in?"

"No, no, you misunderstand me." Gerard spoke quickly and energetically. "It is, I think, a moot question. Should one, if one sees a wrong being done, attempt to put it right? One's interference may do good—but it may do incalculable harm! It is impossible to lay down any ruling on the subject. Some people have a genius for interference—they do it well! Some people do it clumsily and had therefore better leave it alone! Then there is, too, the question of *age*. Young people have the courage of their ideals and convictions—their values are more theoretical than practical. They have not experienced, as yet, that fact contradicts theory! If you have a belief in yourself and in the rightness of what you are doing, you can often accomplish things that are well worth while! (Incidentally, you often do a good deal of harm!) On the other hand, the middle-aged person has experience—he has found that harm as well as, and perhaps more often than good comes of trying to interfere and so—very wisely, he refrains! So the result is even—the earnest young do both harm and good—the prudent middle-aged do neither!"

"All that isn't very helpful," objected Sarah.

"Can one person ever be helpful to another? It is *your* problem, not mine."

44

" You mean *you* are not going to do anything about the Boyntons?"

" No. For me, there would be no chance of success."

" Then there isn't for me, either?"

" For you, there might be."

" Why?"

" Because you have special qualifications. The appeal of your youth and sex."

" Sex? Oh, I see."

" One comes always back to sex, does one not? You have failed with the girl. It does not follow that you would fail with her brother. What you have just told me (what the girl Carol told you) shows very clearly the one menace to Mrs. Boynton's autocracy. The eldest son, Lennox, defied her in the force of his young manhood. He played truant from home, went to local dances. The desire of a man for a mate was stronger than the hypnotic spell. But the old woman was quite aware of the power of sex. (She will have seen something of it in her career.) She dealt with it very cleverly— brought a pretty but penniless girl into the house—encouraged a marriage. And so acquired yet another slave."

Sarah shook her head.

" I don't think young Mrs. Boynton is a slave."

Gerard agreed.

" No, perhaps not. I think that, because she was a quiet, docile young girl, old Mrs. Boynton under-estimated her force of will and character. Nadine Boynton was too young and in-experienced at the time to appreciate the true position. She appreciates it now, but it is too late."

" Do you think she has given up hope?"

Dr. Gerard shook his head doubtfully.

" If she has plans no one would know about them. There are, you know, certain possibilities where Cope is concerned. Man is a naturally jealous animal—and jealousy is a strong force. Lennox Boynton might still be roused from the inertia in which he is sinking."

" And you think "—Sarah purposely made her tone very business-like and professional—" that there's a chance I might be able to do something about Raymond?"

" I do."

Sarah sighed.

" I suppose I might have tried. Oh, well, it's too late now, anyway. And—and I don't like the idea."

45

Gerard looked amused.

"That is because you are English! The English have a complex about sex. They think it is 'not quite nice'."

Sarah's indignant response failed to move him.

"Yes, yes; I know you are very modern—that you use freely in public the most unpleasant words you can find in the dictionary—that you are professional and entirely uninhibited! *Tout de même*, I repeat, you have the same facial characteristics as your mother and your grandmother. You are still the blushing English Miss although you do not blush!"

"I never heard such rubbish!"

Dr. Gerard, a twinkle in his eye, and quite unperturbed, added: "And it makes you very charming."

This time Sarah was speechless.

Dr. Gerard hastily raised his hat. "I take my leave," he said, "before you have time to begin to say all that you think." He escaped into the hotel.

Sarah followed him more slowly.

There was a good deal of activity going on. Several cars loaded with luggage were in process of departing. Lennox and Nadine Boynton and Mr. Cope were standing by a big saloon car superintending arrangements. A fat dragoman was standing talking to Carol with quite unintelligible fluency.

Sarah passed them and went into the hotel.

Mrs. Boynton, wrapped in a thick coat, was sitting in a chair, waiting to depart. Looking at her, a queer revulsion of feeling swept over Sarah. She had felt that Mrs. Boynton was a sinister figure, an incarnation of evil malignancy.

Now, suddenly, she saw the old woman as a pathetic ineffectual figure. To be born with such a lust for power, such a desire for dominion—and to achieve only a petty domestic tyranny! If only her children could see her as Sarah saw her that minute—an object of pity—a stupid, malignant, pathetic, posturing old woman. On an impulse Sarah went up to her.

"Good-bye, Mrs. Boynton," she said. "I hope you'll have a nice trip."

The old lady looked at her. Malignancy struggled with outrage in those eyes.

"You've wanted to be very rude to me," said Sarah.

(Was she crazy, she wondered, what on earth was urging her on to talk like this?)

"You've tried to prevent your son and daughter making

friends with me. Don't you think, really, that that is all very silly and childish? You like to make yourself out a kind of ogre, but really, you know, you're just pathetic and rather ludicrous. If I were you I'd give up all this silly play-acting. I expect you'll hate me for saying this, but I mean it—and some of it may stick. You know you could have a lot of fun still. It's really much better to be—friendly—and kind. You could be if you tried."

There was a pause.

Mrs. Boynton had frozen into a deadly immobility. At last she passed her tongue over her dry lips, her mouth opened. . . . Still for a moment, no words came.

"Go on," said Sarah encouragingly. "Say it! It doesn't matter what you say to me. But think over what I've said to you."

The words came at last—in a soft, husky, but penetrating voice. Mrs. Boynton's basilisk eyes looked, not at Sarah, but oddly over her shoulder. She seemed to address, not Sarah, but some familiar spirit.

"*I never forget,*" she said. "*Remember that. I've never forgotten anything—not an action, not a name, not a face. . . .*"

There was nothing in the words themselves, but the venom with which they were spoken made Sarah retreat a step. And then Mrs. Boynton laughed—it was, definitely, rather a horrible laugh.

Sarah shrugged her shoulders. "You poor old thing," she said.

She turned away. As she went towards the lift she almost collided with Raymond Boynton. On an impulse she spoke quickly.

"Good-bye. I hope you'll have a lovely time. Perhaps we'll meet again some day." She smiled at him, a warm, friendly smile, and passed quickly on.

Raymond stood as though turned to stone. So lost in his own thoughts was he that a small man with big moustaches, endeavouring to pass out of the lift, had to speak several times.

"*Pardon.*"

At last it penetrated. Raymond stepped aside.

"So sorry," he said. "I—I was thinking."

Carol came towards him.

"Ray, get Jinny, will you? She went back to her room. We're going to start."

"Right. I'll tell her she's got to come straight away."

Raymond walked into the lift.

Hercule Poirot stood for a moment looking after him, his eyebrows raised, his head a little on one side as though he was listening.

Then he nodded his head as though in agreement. Walking through the lounge, he took a good look at Carol, who had joined her mother.

Then he beckoned the head waiter who was passing.

"*Pardon*. Can you tell me the name of those people over there?"

"The name is Boynton, monsieur; they are Americans."

"Thank you," said Hercule Poirot.

On the third floor Dr. Gerard, going to his room, passed Raymond Boynton and Ginevra walking towards the waiting lift. Just as they were about to get into it, Ginevra said: "Just a minute, Ray, wait for me in the lift."

She ran back, turned a corner, caught up with the walking man. "Please—I must speak to you."

Dr. Gerard looked up in astonishment.

The girl came up close to him and caught his arm.

"They're taking me away! They may be going to kill me. . . . I don't really belong to them, you know. My name isn't really Boynton. . . ."

She hurried on, her words coming fast and tumbling over each other.

"I'll trust you with the secret. I'm—I'm *Royal*, really! I'm the heiress to a throne. That's why—there are enemies all round me. They try to poison me—all sorts of things. . . . If you could help me—to get away——"

She broke off. Footsteps. "Jinny——"

Beautiful in her sudden startled gesture, the girl put a finger to her lips, threw Gerard an imploring glance, and ran back.

"I'm coming, Ray."

Dr. Gerard walked on with his eyebrows raised. Slowly he shook his head and frowned.

Chapter 10

IT WAS the morning of the start to Petra.

Sarah came down to find a big masterful woman with a rocking-horse nose, whom she had already noticed in the hotel, outside the main entrance, objecting fiercely to the size of the car.

"A great deal too small! Four passengers? *And* a dragoman? Then, of course, we must have a much larger saloon. Please take that car away and return with one of an adequate size."

In vain did the representative of Messrs. Castle's raise his voice in explanation. That was the size of car always provided. It was really a most comfortable car. A larger car was not suitable for desert travel. The large woman, metaphorically speaking, rolled over him like a large steam-roller.

Then she turned her attention to Sarah.

"Miss King? I am Lady Westholme. I am sure you agree with me that that car was grossly inadequate as to size?"

"Well," said Sarah cautiously, "I agree that a larger one *would* be more comfortable!"

The young man from Castle's murmured that a larger car would add to the price.

"The price," said Lady Westholme firmly, "is inclusive, and I shall certainly refuse to sanction any addition to it. Your prospectus distinctly states 'in comfortable saloon car.' You will keep to the terms of your agreement."

Recognising defeat, the young man from Castle's murmured something about seeing what he could do and wilted away from the spot.

Lady Westholme turned to Sarah, a smile of triumph on her weather-beaten countenance, her large red rocking-horse nostrils dilated exultantly.

Lady Westholme was a very well-known figure in the English political world. When Lord Westholme, a middle-aged, simple-minded peer whose only interests in life were hunting, shooting, and fishing, was returning from a trip to the United States, one of his fellow passengers was a Mrs. Vansittart. Shortly afterwards Mrs. Vansittart became Lady Westholme. The match was often cited as one of the examples of the danger of ocean voyages. The new Lady Westholme lived entirely in tweeds and stout brogues, bred dogs, bullied the villagers and forced her husband pitilessly into public life. It being borne in upon her, however, that politics were not Lord Westholme's *métier* in life and never would be, she graciously allowed him to resume his sporting activities and herself stood for Parliament. Being elected with a substantial majority, Lady Westholme threw herself with vigour into political life, being especially active at Question-time. Cartoons of her soon began to appear (always a sure sign of success). As a public figure she stood for the old-fashioned values of family life, welfare work amongst women, and was an ardent supporter of the League of Nations. She had decided views on questions of Agriculture, Housing and Slum Clearance. She was much respected and almost universally disliked! It was highly possible that she would be given an under-secretaryship when her party returned to power. At the moment a Liberal Government (owing to a split in the National Government between Labour and Conservatives) was somewhat unexpectedly in power.

Lady Westholme looked with grim satisfaction after the departing car. " Men always think they can impose upon women," she said.

Sarah thought that it would be a brave man who thought he could impose upon Lady Westholme! She introduced Dr. Gerard, who had just come out of the hotel.

" Your name is, of course, familiar to me," said Lady Westholme, shaking hands. " I was talking to Professor Chantereau the other day in Paris. I have been taking up the question of the treatment of pauper lunatics very strongly lately. Very strongly indeed. Shall we come inside while we wait for a better car to be obtained?"

A vague little middle-aged lady with wisps of grey hair who was hovering nearby turned out to be Miss Amabel Pierce, the fourth member of the party. She, too, was swept into the lounge under Lady Westholme's protecting wing.

" You are a professional woman, Miss King?"

" I've just taken my M.B."

" Good," said Lady Westholme with condescending approval. " If anything is to be accomplished, mark my words, it is women who will do it."

Uneasily conscious for the first time of her sex, Sarah followed Lady Westholme meekly to a seat.

There, as they sat waiting, Lady Westholme informed them that she had refused an invitation to stay with the High Commissioner during her stay in Jerusalem. " I did not want to be hampered by officialdom. I wished to look into things for myself."

" What things?" Sarah wondered.

Lady Westholme went on to explain that she was staying at the Solomon Hotel so as to remain unhampered. She added that she had made several suggestions to the manager for the more competent running of his hotel.

" Efficiency," said Lady Westholme, " is my watchword."

It certainly seemed to be! In a quarter of an hour a large and extremely comfortable car arrived and in due course— after advice from Lady Westholme as to how the luggage should be bestowed—the party set off.

Their first halt was the Dead Sea. They had lunch at Jericho. Afterwards when Lady Westholme, armed with a Baedeker, had gone off with Miss Pierce, the doctor and the fat dragoman, to do a tour of old Jericho, Sarah remained in the garden of the hotel.

Her head ached slightly and she wanted to be alone. A deep depression weighed her down—a depression for which she found it hard to account. She felt suddenly listless and un-interested, disinclined for sightseeing, bored by her com-panions. She wished at this moment that she had never com-mitted herself to this Petra tour. It was going to be very expensive and she felt quite sure she wasn't going to enjoy it! Lady Westholme's booming voice, Miss Pierce's endless twit-terings, and the anti-Zionist lamentation of the dragoman, were already fraying her nerves to a frazzle. She disliked almost as much Dr. Gerard's amused air of knowing exactly how she was feeling.

She wondered where the Boyntons were now—perhaps they had gone on to Syria—they might be at Baalbek or Damascus. Raymond—she wondered what Raymond was doing. Strange how clearly she could see his face—its eagerness—its diffidence —its nervous tension. . . .

Oh, hell! Why go on thinking of people she would pro-bably never see again? That scene the other day with the old woman—what could have possessed her to march up to the old lady and spurt out a lot of nonsense. Other people must have heard some of it. She fancied that Lady Westholme had been quite close by. Sarah tried to remember exactly what it was she had said. Something that probably sounded quite absurdly hysterical. Goodness, what a fool she has made of herself! But it wasn't her fault really; it was old Mrs. Boynton's. There was something about her that made you lose your sense of proportion.

Dr. Gerard entered and plumped down in a chair, wiping his hot forehead.

"Phew! That woman should be poisoned!" he declared.

Sarah started. "Mrs. Boynton?"

"Mrs. Boynton! No, I meant that Lady Westholme! It is incredible to me that she has had a husband for many years and that he has not already done so. What can he be made of, that husband?"

Sarah laughed.

"Oh, he's the 'huntin', fishin', shootin'' kind," she explained.

"Psychologically that is very sound! He appeases his lust to kill on the (so-called) lower creations."

"I believe he is very proud of his wife's activities."

The Frenchman suggested:

"Because they take her a good deal away from home? That is understandable." Then he went on, "What did you say just now? Mrs. Boynton? Undoubtedly it would be a very good idea to poison her, too. Undeniably the simplest solution of that family problem! In fact a great many women would be better poisoned. All women who have grown old and ugly."

He made an expressive face.

Sarah cried out, laughing:

"Oh, you Frenchmen! You've got no use for any woman who isn't young and attractive."

Gerard shrugged his shoulders.

"We are more honest about it, that is all. Englishmen, they do not get up in tubes and trains for ugly women—no, no."

"How depressing life is," said Sarah with a sigh.

"There is no need for *you* to sigh, mademoiselle."

"Well, I feel thoroughly disgruntled to-day."

"Naturally."

"What do you mean—naturally?" snapped Sarah.

"You could find the reason very easily if you examine your state of mind honestly."

"I think it's our fellow-travellers who depress me," said

52

Sarah. "It's awful, isn't it, but I do hate women! When they're inefficient and idiotic like Miss Pierce, they infuriate me—and, when they're efficient like Lady Westholme, they annoy me more still."

"It is, I should say, unavoidable that these two people should annoy you. Lady Westholme is exactly fitted to the life she leads and is completely happy and successful. Miss Pierce has worked for years as a nursery governess and has suddenly come into a small legacy which has enabled her to fulfil her life-long wish and travel. So far, travel has lived up to her expectations. Consequently you, who have just been thwarted in obtaining what you want, naturally resent the existence of people who have been more successful in life than you are."

"I suppose you're right," said Sarah gloomily. "What a horribly accurate mind-reader you are. I keep trying to humbug myself and you won't let me."

At this moment the others returned. The guide seemed the most exhausted of the three. He was quite subdued and hardly exuded any information on the way to Amman. He did not even mention the Jews. For which everyone was profoundly grateful. His voluble and frenzied account of their iniquities had done much to try everyone's temper on the journey from Jerusalem.

Now the road wound upward from the Jordan, twisting and turning, with clumps of oleanders showing rose-coloured flowers.

They reached Amman late in the afternoon and after a short visit to the Græco-Roman theatre went to bed early. They were to make an early start the next morning as it was a full day's motor run across the desert to Ma'an.

They left soon after eight o'clock. The party was inclined to be silent. It was a hot airless day and by noon when a halt was made for a picnic lunch to be eaten, it was really stiflingly hot. The irritation of a hot day of being boxed up closely with three other human beings had got a little on everyone's nerves.

Lady Westholme and Dr. Gerard had a somewhat irritable argument over the League of Nations. Lady Westholme was a fervent supporter of the League. The Frenchman, on the other hand, chose to be witty at the League's expense. From the attitude of the League concerning Abyssinia and Spain they passed to the Litvania boundary dispute of which Sarah had never heard and from there to the activities of the League in suppressing dope gangs.

"You must admit they have done wonderful work. Wonderful!" snapped Lady Westholme.

Dr. Gerard shrugged his shoulders.

"Perhaps. And at wonderful expense too!"

"The matter is a very serious one. Under the Dangerous Drugs Act——" The argument waged on.

Miss Pierce twittered to Sarah: "It is really *most* interesting travelling with Lady Westholme."

Sarah said acidly: "Is it?" but Miss Pierce did not notice the acerbity and twittered happily on.

"I've so *often* seen her name in the papers. So *clever* of women to go into public life and hold their own. I'm always so *glad* when a *woman* accomplishes something!"

"Why?" demanded Sarah ferociously.

Miss Pierce's mouth fell open and she stammered a little.

"Oh, because—I mean—just because—well—it's so nice that women are *able* to do things!"

"I don't agree," said Sarah. "It's nice when *any* human being is able to accomplish something worth while! It doesn't matter a bit whether it's a man or a woman. Why should it?"

"Well, of course——" said Miss Pierce. "Yes—I confess —of course, looking at it in that light——"

But she looked slightly wistful. Sarah said more gently:

"I'm sorry, but I do hate this differentiation between the sexes. '*The modern girl has a thoroughly business-like attitude towards life.*' That sort of thing. It's not a bit true! Some girls are business-like and some aren't. Some men are sentimental and muddle-headed, others are clear-headed and logical. There are just different types of brains. Sex only matters where sex is directly concerned."

Miss Pierce flushed a little at the word sex and adroitly changed the subject.

"One can't help wishing that there were a little shade," she murmured. "But I do think all this emptiness is so wonderful, don't you?"

Sarah nodded.

Yes, she thought, the emptiness was marvellous.... Healing.... Peaceful.... No human being to agitate one with their tiresome inter-relationships.... No burning personal problems! Now, at last, she felt, she was free of the Boyntons. Free of that strange compelling wish to interfere in the lives of people whose orbit did not remotely touch her own. She felt soothed and at peace. Here was loneliness, emptiness, spaciousness. . . . In fact, peace. . . .

Only, of course, one wasn't alone to enjoy it. Lady Westholme and Dr. Gerard had finished with drugs and were now arguing about guileless young women who were exported in a sinister manner to Argentinian cabarets. Dr. Gerard had displayed throughout the conversation a levity which Lady Westholme, who, being a true politician, had no sense of humour, found definitely deplorable.

" We go on now, yes?" announced the tarbushed dragoman, and began to talk about the iniquities of Jews again.

It was about an hour off sunset when they reached Ma'an at last. Strange wild-faced men crowded round the car. After a short halt they went on.

Looking over the flat desert country, Sarah was at a loss as to where the rocky stronghold of Petra could be. Surely they could see for miles and miles all round them? There were no mountains, no hills anywhere. Were they, then, still many miles from their journey's end?

They reached the village of Ain Musa where the cars were to be left. Here horses were waiting for them—sorry-looking thin beasts. The inadequacy of her striped washing-frock disturbed Miss Pierce greatly. Lady Westholme was sensibly attired in riding breeches, not perhaps a particularly becoming style to her type of figure, but certainly practical.

The horses were led out of the village along a slippery path with loose stones. The ground fell away and the horses zigzagged down. The sun was close on setting.

Sarah was very tired with the long, hot journey in the car. Her senses felt dazed. The ride was like a dream. It seemed to her afterwards that it was like the pit of Hell opening at one's feet. The way wound down—down into the ground. The shapes of rock rose up round them—down, down into the bowels of the earth, through a labyrinth of red cliffs. They towered now on either side. Sarah felt stifled—menaced by the ever-narrowing gorge.

She thought confusedly to herself: " Down into the valley of death—down into the valley of death. . . ."

On and on. It grew dark—the vivid red of the walls faded—and still on, winding in and out, imprisoned, lost in the bowels of the earth.

She thought: "It's fantastic and unbelievable . . . a dead city."

And again like a refrain came the words: "*The valley of death. . . .*"

Lanterns were lit now. The horses wound along through the narrow ways. Suddenly they came out into a wide space—the cliffs receded. Far ahead of them were a cluster of lights.

"That is camp!" said the guide.

The horses quickened their pace a little—not very much—they were too starved and dispirited for that, but they showed just a shade of enthusiasm. Now the way ran along a gravelly water-bed. The lights grew nearer.

They could see a cluster of tents, a higher row up against the face of a cliff. Caves, too, hollowed out in the rock.

They were arriving. Bedouin servants came running out.

Sarah stared up at one of the caves. It held a sitting figure. What was it? An idol? A gigantic squatting image?

No, that was the flickering lights that made it loom so large. But it *must* be an idol of some kind, sitting there immovable, brooding over the place. . . .

And then, suddenly her heart gave a leap of recognition.

Gone was the feeling of peace—of escape—that the desert had given her. She had been led from freedom back into captivity. She had ridden down into this dark winding valley and here, like an arch priestess of some forgotten cult, like a monstrous swollen female Buddha, sat Mrs. Boynton. . . .

Chapter 11

MRS. BOYNTON was here, at Petra!

Sarah answered mechanically questions that were addressed to her. Would she have dinner straight away—it was ready—or would she like to wash first? Would she prefer to sleep in a tent or a cave?

Her answer to that came quickly. A tent. She flinched at the thought of a cave, the vision of that monstrous squatting figure recurred to her. (Why was it that something about the woman seemed hardly human?)

Finally she followed one of the native servants. He wore khaki breeches much patched and untidy puttees and a ragged coat very much the worse for wear. On his head the native headdress, the cheffiyah, its long folds protecting the neck and secured in place with a black silk twist fitting tightly to the crown of his head. Sarah admired the easy swing with which he walked—the careless proud carriage of his head. Only the European part of his costume seemed tawdry and wrong. She thought: " Civilisation *is* all wrong—*all* wrong! But for civilisation there wouldn't be a Mrs. Boynton! In savage tribes they'd probably have killed and eaten her years ago!"

She realised, half-humorously, that she was over-tired and on edge. A wash in hot water and a dusting of powder over her face and she felt herself again—cool, poised, and ashamed of her recent panic.

She passed a comb through her thick black hair, squinting sideways at her reflection in the wavering light of a small oil-lamp in a very inadequate glass.

Then she pushed aside the tent-flap and came out into the night prepared to descend to the big marquee below.

" You—here?"

It was a low cry—dazed, incredulous.

She turned to look straight into Raymond Boynton's eyes. So amazed they were! And something in them held her silent and almost afraid. Such an unbelievable joy. . . . It was as though he had seen a vision of Paradise—wondering, dazed, thankful, humble! Never, in all her life, was Sarah to forget that look. So might the damned look up and see Paradise. . . .

He said again: " *You. . . .*"

It did something to her—that low, vibrant tone. It made her heart turn over in her breast. It made her feel shy, afraid, humble and yet suddenly arrogantly glad. She said quite simply: " Yes."

He came nearer—still dazed—still only half believing.

Then suddenly he took her hand.

" It *is* you," he said. " You're real. I thought at first you were a ghost—because I'd been thinking about you so much." He paused and then said, " I love you, you know. . . . I have from the moment I saw you in the train. I know that now. And I want you to know it so that—so that you'll know it isn't me—the real me—who—who behaves so caddishly. You see I can't answer for myself even now. I might do—anything! I might pass you by or cut you, but I do want you to know that it isn't me—the real me—who is responsible for that. It's my nerves. I can't depend on them. . . . When She tells me to
57

do things—I do them! My nerves make me! You will understand, won't you? Despise me if you have to——"

She interrupted him. Her voice was low and unexpectedly
sweet. " I won't despise you."

" All the same, I'm pretty despicable! I ought to—to be
able to behave like a man."

It was partly an echo of Gerard's advice, but more out of
her own knowledge and hope that Sarah answered—and
behind the sweetness of her voice there was a ring of certainty
and conscious authority.

" You will now."

" Shall I?" His voice was wistful. " Perhaps. . . ."

" You'll have courage now. I'm sure of it."

He drew himself up—flung back his head.

" Courage? Yes, that's all that's needed. Courage!"

Suddenly he bent his head, touched her hand with his lips.
A minute later he had left her.

Chapter 12

SARAH WENT down to the big marquee. She found her three
fellow-travellers there. They were sitting at table eating. The
guide was explaining that there was another party here.

" They came two days ago. Go day after to-morrow.
Americans. The mother, very fat, very difficult get here!
Carried in chair by bearers—they say very hard work—they
get very hot—yes."

Sarah gave a sudden spurt of laughter. Of course, take it
properly, the whole thing was funny!

The fat dragoman looked at her gratefully. He was not
finding his task too easy. Lady Westholme had contradicted
him out of Baedeker three times that day and had now found
fault with the type of bed provided. He was grateful to the
one member of his party who seemed to be unaccountably in
a good temper.

" Ha!" said Lady Westholme. " I think these people were
at the Solomon. I recognised the old mother as we arrived
here. I think I saw you talking to her at the hotel, Miss
King."

Sarah blushed guiltily, hoping Lady Westholme had not
overheard much of that conversation.

"Really, what possessed me!" she thought to herself in an agony.

In the meantime Lady Westholme had made a pronouncement. "Not interesting people at all. Very provincial," she said.

Miss Pierce made eager sycophantish noises and Lady Westholme embarked on a history of various interesting and prominent Americans whom she had met recently.

The weather being so unusually hot for the time of year, an early start was arranged for the morrow.

The four assembled for breakfast at six o'clock. There were no signs of any of the Boynton family. After Lady Westholme had commented unfavourably on the absence of fruit, they consumed tea, tinned milk, and fried eggs in a generous allowance of fat flanked by extremely salt bacon.

Then they started forth, Lady Westholme and Dr. Gerard discussing with animation on the part of the former the exact value of vitamins in diet and the proper nutrition of the working classes.

Then there was a sudden hail from the camp and they halted to allow another person to join the party. It was Mr. Jefferson Cope who hurried after them, his pleasant face flushed with the exertion of running.

"Why, if you don't mind, I'd like to join your party this morning. Good morning, Miss King. Quite a surprise meeting you and Dr. Gerard here. What do you think of it?"

He made a gesture indicating the fantastic red rocks that stretched in every direction.

"I think it's rather wonderful and just a little horrible," said Sarah. "I always thought of it as romantic and dream-like —the 'rose-red city.' But it's much more *real* than that—it's as real as—as raw beef."

"And very much the colour of it," agreed Mr. Cope.

"But it's marvellous, too," admitted Sarah.

The party began to climb. Two Bedouin guides accompanied them. Tall men, with an easy carriage, they swung upward unconcernedly in their hobnailed boots completely footsure on the slippery slope. Difficulties soon began. Sarah had a good head for heights and so had Dr. Gerard. But both Mr. Cope and Lady Westholme were far from happy, and the unfortunate Miss Pierce had to be almost carried over the precipitous places, her eyes shut, her face green, while her voice rose ceaselessly in a perpetual wail.

" I never could look down places. Never—from a child!"

Once she declared her intention of going back, but on turning to face the descent, her skin assumed an even greener tinge, and she reluctantly decided that to go on was the only thing to be done.

Dr. Gerard was kind and reassuring. He went up behind her, holding a stick between her and the sheer drop like a balustrade and she confessed that the illusion of a rail did much to conquer the feeling of vertigo.

Sarah, panting a little, asked the dragoman, Mahmoud, who, in spite of his ample proportions, showed no signs of distress:

" Don't you ever have trouble getting people up here? Elderly ones, I mean."

" Always—always we have trouble," agreed Mahmoud serenely.

" Do you always try and take them?"

Mahmoud shrugged his thick shoulders.

" They like to come. They have paid money to see these things. They wish to see them. The Bedouin guides are very clever—very sure-footed—always they manage."

They arrived at last at the summit. Sarah drew a deep breath.

All around and below stretched the blood-red rocks—a strange and unbelievable country unparalleled anywhere. Here in the exquisite pure morning air they stood like gods, surveying a baser world—a world of flaring violence.

Here was, as the guide told them, the ' Place of Sacrifice ' —the ' High Place.' He showed them the trough cut in the flat rock at their feet.

Sarah strayed away from the rest, from the glib phrases that flowed so readily from the dragoman's tongue. She sat on a rock, pushed her hands through her thick black hair, and gazed down on the world at her feet. Presently she was aware of someone standing by her side. Dr. Gerard's voice said:

" You appreciate the appositeness of the devil's temptation in the New Testament. Satan took Our Lord up to the summit of a mountain and showed Him the world. ' All these things will I give thee, if thou wilt fall down and worship me.' How much greater the temptation up on high to be a God of Material Power."

Sarah assented, but her thoughts were so clearly elsewhere that Gerard observed her in some surprise.

"You are pondering something very deeply," he said.

"Yes, I am." She turned a perplexed face to him. "It's a wonderful idea—to have a place of sacrifice up here. I think sometimes, don't you, that a sacrifice is *necessary*. . . . I mean, one can have too much regard for life. Death isn't really so important as we make out."

"If you feel that Miss King, you should not have adopted our profession. To us, Death is and must always be—the Enemy."

Sarah shivered.

"Yes, I suppose you're right. And yet, so often death might solve a problem. It might mean, even, fuller life. . . ."

"It is expedient for us that one man should die for the people!" quoted Gerard gravely.

Sarah turned a startled face on him.

"I didn't mean——" She broke off. Jefferson Cope was approaching them.

"Now this is really a most remarkable spot," he declared. "Most remarkable, and I'm only too pleased not to have missed it. I don't mind confessing that though Mrs. Boynton is certainly a most remarkable woman—I greatly admire her pluck in being determined to come here—it does certainly complicate matters travelling with her. Her health is poor, and I suppose it naturally makes her a little inconsiderate of other people's feelings, but it does not seem to occur to her that her family might like occasionally to go on excursions without her. She's just so used to them clustering round her that I suppose she doesn't think——"

Mr. Cope broke off. His nice kindly face looked a little disturbed and uncomfortable.

"You know," he said, "I heard a piece of information about Mrs. Boynton that disturbed me greatly."

Sarah was lost in her own thoughts again—Mr. Cope's voice just flowed pleasantly in her ears like the agreeable murmur of a remote stream, but Dr. Gerard said:

"Indeed? What was it?"

"My informant was a lady I came across in the hotel at Tiberias. It concerned a servant girl who had been in Mrs. Boynton's employ. The girl, I gather, was—had——"

Mr. Cope paused, glanced delicately at Sarah and lowered his voice. "She was going to have a child. The old lady, it seemed, discovered this, but was apparently quite kind to the girl. Then a few weeks before the child was born she turned her out of the house."

Dr. Gerard's eyebrows went up.

" Ah," he said reflectively.

" My informant seemed very positive of her facts. I don't know whether you agree with me, but that seems to me a very cruel and heartless thing to do. I cannot under-stand——"

Dr. Gerard interrupted him.

" You should try to. That incident, I have no doubt, gave Mrs. Boynton a good deal of quiet enjoyment."

Mr. Cope turned a shocked face on him.

" No, sir," he said with emphasis. " That I cannot believe. Such an idea is quite inconceivable."

Softly Dr. Gerard quoted:

" *So I returned and did consider all the oppressions done beneath the sun. And there was weeping and wailing from those that were oppressed and had no comfort ; for with their oppressors there was power, so that no one came to comfort them. Then I did praise the dead which are already dead, yea, more than the living which linger still in life ; yea, he that is not is better than dead or living ; for he doth not know of the evil that is wrought for ever on earth. . . .*"

He broke off and said:

" My dear sir, I have made a life's study of the strange things that go on in the human mind. It is no good turning one's face only to the fairer side of life. Below the decencies and conventions of everyday life, there lies a vast reservoir of strange things. There is such a thing, for instance, as delight in cruelty for its own sake. But when you have found that, there is something deeper still. The desire, profound and pitiful, to be appreciated. If that is thwarted, if through an unpleasing personality a human being is unable to get the response it needs, it turns to other methods—it must be *felt* —it must *count*—and so to innumerable strange perversions. The habit of cruelty, like any other habit, can be cultivated, can take hold of one——"

Mr. Cope coughed. " I think, Dr. Gerard, that you are slightly exaggerating. Really, the air up here is too wonderful. . . ."

He edged away. Gerard smiled a little. He looked again at Sarah. She was frowning—her face was set in a youthful sternness. She looked, he thought, like a young judge delivering sentence. . . .

He turned as Miss Pierce tripped unsteadily towards him.

" We are going down now," she fluttered. " Oh dear! I am sure I shall never manage it, but the guide says the way down is quite a different route and much easier. I do hope so, because from a child I never have been able to look down from heights. . . ."

The descent was down the course of a waterfall. Although there were loose stones which were a possible source of danger to ankles, it presented no dizzy vistas.

The party arrived back at the camp weary but in good spirits and with an excellent appetite for a late lunch. It was past two o'clock.

The Boynton family was sitting round the big table in the marquee. They were just finishing their meal.

Lady Westholme addressed a gracious sentence to them in her most condescending manner.

" Really a most interesting morning," she said. " Petra is a wonderful spot."

Carol, to whom the words seemed addressed, shot a quick look at her mother and murmured:

" Oh, yes—yes, it is," and relapsed into silence.

Lady Westholme, feeling she had done her duty, addressed herself to her food.

As they ate, the four discussed plans for the afternoon.

" I think I shall rest most of the afternoon," said Miss Pierce. " It is important, I think, not to do too much."

" I shall go for a walk and explore," said Sarah. " What about you, Dr. Gerard?"

" I will go with you."

Mrs. Boynton dropped a spoon with a ringing clatter and everyone jumped.

" I think," said Lady Westholme, " that I shall follow your example, Miss Pierce. Perhaps half an hour with a book, then I shall lie down and take an hour's rest at least. After that, perhaps, a short stroll."

Slowly, with the help of Lennox, old Mrs. Boynton struggled to her feet. She stood for a moment and then spoke.

" You'd better all go for a walk this afternoon," she said with unexpected amiability.

It was, perhaps, slightly ludicrous to see the startled faces of her family.

"But, Mother, what about you?"

"I don't need any of you. I like sitting alone with my book. Jinny had better not go. She'll lie down and have a sleep."

"Mother, I'm not tired. I want to go with the others."

"You *are* tired. You've got a headache! You must be careful of yourself. Go and lie down and sleep. I know what's best for you."

"I—I——"

Her head thrown back, the girl stared rebelliously. Then her eyes dropped—faltered. . . .

"Silly child," said Mrs. Boynton. "Go to your tent."

She stumped out of the marquee—the others followed.

"Dear me," said Miss Pierce. "What very peculiar people. Such a very odd colour—the mother. Quite purple. Heart, I should imagine. The heat must be very trying to her."

Sarah thought: "She's letting them go free this afternoon. She knows Raymond wants to be with me. Why? Is it a trap?"

After lunch, when she had gone to her tent and had changed into a fresh linen dress, the thought still worried her. Since last night her feeling towards Raymond had swelled into a passion of protective tenderness. This, then, was love—this agony on another's behalf—this desire to avert, at all costs, pain from the beloved. . . . Yes, she loved Raymond Boynton. It was St. George and the Dragon reversed. It was she who was the rescuer and Raymond who was the chained victim.

And Mrs. Boynton was the Dragon. A dragon whose sudden amiability was, to Sarah's suspicious mind, definitely sinister.

It was about a quarter-past-three when Sarah strolled down to the marquee.

Lady Westholme was sitting on a chair. Despite the heat of the day she was still wearing her serviceable Harris tweed skirt. On her lap was the report of a Royal Commission. Dr. Gerard was talking to Miss Pierce, who was standing by her tent holding a book entitled *The Love Quest* and described on its wrapper as a thrilling tale of passion and misunderstanding.

"I don't think it's wise to lie down too soon after lunch," explained Miss Pierce. "One's digestion, you know. Quite cool and pleasant in the shadow of the marquee. Oh dear, do you think that old lady is wise to sit in the sun up there?"

They all looked at the ridge in front of them. Mrs. Boynton was sitting as she had sat last night, a motionless Buddha in the door of her cave. There was no other human creature in sight. All the camp personnel were asleep. A short distance away, following the line of the valley, a little group of people walked together.

" For once," said Dr. Gerard, " the good Mamma permits them to enjoy themselves without her. A new devilment on her part, perhaps?"

" Do you know," said Sarah, " that's just what I thought."

" What suspicious minds we have. Come, let us join the truants."

Leaving Miss Pierce to her exciting reading, they set off. Once round the bend of the valley, they caught up the other party who were walking slowly. For once, the Boyntons looked happy and carefree.

Lennox and Nadine, Carol and Raymond, Mr. Cope with a broad smile on his face and the last arrivals, Gerard and Sarah, were soon all laughing and talking together.

A sudden wild hilarity was born. In everyone's mind was the feeling that this was a snatched pleasure—a stolen joy to enjoy to the full. Sarah and Raymond did not draw apart. Instead, Sarah walked with Carol and Lennox. Dr. Gerard chatted to Raymond close behind them. Nadine and Jefferson Cope walked a little apart.

It was the Frenchman who broke up the party. His words had been coming spasmodically for some time. Suddenly he stopped.

" A thousand excuses. I fear I must go back."

Sarah looked at him. " Anything the matter?"

He nodded. " Yes, fever. It's been coming on ever since lunch."

Sarah scrutinised him. " Malaria?"

" Yes. I'll go back and take quinine. Hope this won't be a bad attack. It is a legacy from a visit to the Congo."

" Shall I come with you?" asked Sarah.

" No, no. I have my case of drugs with me. A confounded nuisance. Go on, all of you."

He walked quickly back in the direction of the camp.

Sarah looked undecidedly after him for a minute, then she met Raymond's eyes, smiled at him, and the Frenchman was forgotten.

For a time the six of them, Carol, herself, Lennox, Mr. Cope, Nadine and Raymond, kept together.

Then, somehow or other, she and Raymond had drifted apart. They walked on, climbing up rocks, turning ledges, and rested at last in a shady spot.

There was a silence—then Raymond said:

" What's your name? It's King, I know. But your other name."

" Sarah."

" Sarah. May I call you that?"

" Of course."

" Sarah, will you tell me something about yourself?"

Leaning back against the rocks, she talked, telling him of her life at home in Yorkshire, of her dogs and the aunt who had brought her up.

Then, in his turn, Raymond told her a little, disjointedly, of his own life.

After that there was a long silence. Their hands strayed together. They sat, like children, hand in hand, strangely content.

Then, as the sun grew lower, Raymond stirred.

" I'm going back now," he said. " No, not with you. I want to go back by myself. There's something I have to say and do. Once that's done, once I've proved to myself that I'm not a coward—then—then—I shan't be ashamed to come to you and ask you to help me. I shall need help, you know. I shall probably have to borrow money from you."

Sarah smiled.

" I'm glad you're a realist. You can count on me."

" But first I've got to do this alone."

" Do what?"

The young boyish face grew suddenly stern. Raymond Boynton said: " I've got to prove my courage. It's now or never."

Then, abruptly, he turned and strode away.

Sarah leant back against the rock and watched his receding figure. Something in his words had vaguely alarmed her. He had seemed so intense—so terribly in earnest and strung up. For a moment she wished she had gone with him. . . .

But she rebuked herself sternly for that wish. Raymond had desired to stand alone, to test his new-found courage. That was his right.

66

But she prayed with all her heart that that courage would not fail. . . .

The sun was setting when Sarah came once more in sight of the camp. As she came nearer in the dim light she could make out the grim figure of Mrs. Boynton still sitting in the mouth of the cave. Sarah shivered a little at the sight of that grim, motionless figure. . . .

She hurried past on the path below and came into the lighted marquee.

Lady Westholme was sitting knitting a navy-blue jumper, a skein of wool hung round her neck. Miss Pierce was embroidering a table-mat with anæmic blue forget-me-nots, and being instructed on the proper reform of the Divorce Laws.

The servants came in and out preparing for the evening meal. The Boyntons were at the far end of the marquee in deck-chairs reading. Mahmoud appeared, fat and dignified, and was plaintively reproachful. Very nice after-tea ramble had been arranged to take place, but everyone absent from camp. . . . The programme was now entirely thrown out. . . . Very instructive visit to Nabatæn architecture.

Sarah said hastily that they had all enjoyed themselves very much.

She went off to her tent to wash for supper. On the way back she paused by Dr. Gerard's tent, calling in a low voice: " Dr. Gerard."

There was no answer. She lifted the flap and looked in. The doctor was lying motionless on his bed. Sarah withdrew noiselessly, hoping he was asleep.

A servant came to her and pointed to the marquee. Evidently supper was ready. She strolled down again. Everyone else was assembled there round the table with the exception of Dr. Gerard and Mrs. Boynton. A servant was despatched to tell the old lady dinner was ready. Then there was a sudden commotion outside. Two frightened servants rushed in and spoke excitedly to the dragoman in Arabic.

Mahmoud looked round him in a flustered manner and went outside. On an impulse Sarah joined him.

" What's the matter?" she asked.

Mahmoud replied: " The old lady. Abdul says she is ill— cannot move."

" I'll come and see."

Sarah quickened her step. Following Mahmoud, she climbed the rock and walked along until she came to the squat figure in the chair, touched the puffy hand, felt for the pulse, bent over her. . . .

When she straightened herself she was paler.

She retraced her steps back to the marquee. In the doorway she paused a minute looking at the group at the far end of the table. Her voice when she spoke sounded to herself brusque and unnatural.

" I'm so sorry," she said. She forced herself to address the head of the family, Lennox. "*Your mother is dead, Mr. Boynton.*"

And curiously, as though from a great distance, she watched the faces of five people to whom that announcement meant freedom. . . .

PART II

Chapter One

COLONEL CARBURY smiled across the table at his guest and raised his glass. " Well, here's to crime ! "

Hercule Poirot's eyes twinkled in acknowledgment of the aptness of the toast.

He had come to Amman with a letter of introduction to Colonel Carbury from Colonel Race.

Carbury had been interested to see this world-famous person to whose gifts his old friend and ally in the Intelligence had paid such unstinting tribute.

" As neat a bit of psychological deduction as you'll ever find ! " Race had written of the solution of the Shaitana murder.

" We must show you all we can of the neighbourhood," said Carbury, twisting a somewhat ragged brindled moustache. He was an untidy stocky man of medium height with a semi-bald head and vague, mild, blue eyes. He did not look in the least like a soldier. He did not look even particularly alert. He was not in the least one's idea of a disciplinarian. Yet in Transjordania he was a power.

" There's Jerash," he said. " Care about that sort of thing?"

" I am interested in everything ! "

" Yes," said Carbury. " That's the only way to react to life." He paused.

" Tell me, d'you ever find your own special job has a way of following you round?"

" Pardon?"

" Well—to put it plainly—do you come to places expecting a holiday from crime—and find instead bodies cropping up?"

" It has happened, yes ; more than once."

" H'm," said Colonel Carbury and looked particularly abstracted.

69

Then he roused himself with a jerk. "Got a body now I'm not very happy about," he said.

"Indeed?"

"Yes. Here in Amman. Old American woman. Went to Petra with her family. Trying journey, unusual heat for time of year, old woman suffered from heart trouble, difficulties of the journey a bit harder for her than she imagined, extra strain on heart—she popped off!"

"Here—in Amman?"

"No, down at Petra. They brought the body here to-day."

"Ah!"

"All quite natural. Perfectly possible. Likeliest thing in the world to happen. Only——"

"Yes? Only——?"

Colonel Carbury scratched his bald head.

"I've got the idea," he said, "that her family did her in!"

"Aha! And what makes you think that?"

Colonel Carbury did not reply to that question directly.

"Unpleasant old woman, it seems. No loss. General feeling all round that her popping off was a good thing. Anyway, very difficult to prove anything so long as the family stick together and if necessary lie like hell. One doesn't want complications—or international unpleasantness. Easiest thing to do—let it go! Nothing really to go upon. Knew a doctor chap once. He told me—often had suspicions in cases of his patients—hurried into the next world a little ahead of time! *He* said—best thing to do to keep quiet unless you really had something damned good to go upon! Otherwise beastly stink, case not proved, black mark against an earnest hard-working G.P. Something in that. All the same——" He scratched his head again. "I'm a tidy man," he said unexpectedly.

Colonel Carbury's tie was under his left ear, his socks were wrinkled, his coat stained and torn. Yet Hercule Poirot did not smile. He saw, clearly enough, the inner neatness of Colonel Carbury's mind, his neatly docketed facts, his carefully sorted impressions.

"Yes. I'm a tidy man," said Carbury. He waved a vague hand. "Don't like a mess. When I come across a mess I want to clear it up. See?"

Hercule Poirot nodded gravely. He saw.

"There was no doctor down there?" he asked.

"Yes, two. One of 'em was down with malaria, though. The other's a girl—just out of the medical student stage. Still, she knows her job, I suppose. There wasn't anything odd about the death. Old woman had got a dicky heart. She'd been taking heart medicine for some time. Nothing really surprising about her conking out suddenly like she did."

"Then what, my friend, is worrying you?" asked Poirot gently.

Colonel Carbury turned a harassed blue eye on him.

"Heard of a Frenchman called Gerard? Theodore Gerard?"

"Certainly. A very distinguished man in his own line."

"Loony bins," confirmed Colonel Carbury. "Passion for a charwoman at the age of four makes you insist you're the Archbishop of Canterbury when you're thirty-eight. Can't see why and never have, but these chaps explain it very convincingly."

"Dr. Gerard is certainly an authority on certain forms of deep-seated neurosis," agreed Poirot, with a smile. "Is—er—are—er—his views on the happening at Petra based on that line of argument?"

Colonel Carbury shook his head vigorously.

"No, no. Shouldn't have worried about them if they had been! Not, mind you, that I don't believe it's all true. It's just one of those things I don't understand—like one of my Bedouin fellows who can get out of a car in the middle of a flat desert, feel the ground with his hand and tell you to within a mile or two where you are. It isn't magic, but it looks like it. No, Dr. Gerard's story is quite straightforward. Just plain facts. I think, if you're interested—you *are* interested?"

"Yes, yes."

"Good man. Then I think I'll just phone over and get Gerard along here, and you can hear his story for yourself."

When the Colonel had despatched an orderly on this quest, Poirot said:

"Of what does this family consist?"

"Name's Boynton. There are two sons, one of 'em married. His wife's a nice-looking girl—the quiet, sensible kind. And there are two daughters. Both of 'em quite good-looking in totally different styles. Younger one a bit nervy—but that may be just shock."

"Boynton," said Poirot. His eyebrows rose. "That is curious—very curious."

Carbury cocked an inquiring eye at him. But as Poirot said nothing more, he himself went on:

"Seems pretty obvious Mother was a pest! Had to be waited on hand and foot and kept the whole lot of them dancing attendance. And she held the purse strings. None of them had a penny of their own."

"Aha! All very interesting. Is it known how she left her money?"

"I did just slip that question in—casual like, you know. It gets divided equally between the lot of them."

Poirot nodded his head. Then he asked:

"You are of opinion that they are all in it?"

"Don't know. That's where the difficulty's going to lie. Whether it was a concerted effort, or whether it was one bright member's idea—I don't know. Maybe the whole thing's a mare's nest! What it comes to is this: I'd like to have your professional opinion. Ah, here comes Gerard."

Chapter 2

THE Frenchman came in with a quick yet unhurried tread. As he shook hands with Colonel Carbury he shot a keen, interested glance at Poirot. Carbury said:

"This is M. Hercule Poirot. Staying with me. Been talking to him about this business down at Petra."

"Ah, yes?" Gerard's quick eyes looked Poirot up and down. "You are interested?"

Hercule Poirot threw up his hands.

"Alas! one is always incurably interested in one's own subject."

"True," said Gerard.

"Have a drink?" said Carbury.

He poured out a whisky and soda and placed it by Gerard's elbow. He held up the decanter inquiringly, but Poirot shook his head. Colonel Carbury set it down again and drew his chair a little nearer.

"Well," he said, "where are we?"

"I gather," said Poirot to Gerard, "that Colonel Carbury is not satisfied."

Gerard made an expressive gesture.

"And that," he said, "is my fault! And I may be wrong. Remember that, Colonel Carbury, I may be entirely wrong."

Carbury gave a grunt.

" Give Poirot the facts," he said.

Dr. Gerard began by a brief recapitulation of the events preceding the journey to Petra. He gave a short sketch of the various members of the Boynton family and described the condition of emotional strain under which they were labouring.

Poirot listend with interest.

Then Gerard proceeded to the actual events of their first day at Petra, describing how he had returned to the camp.

" I was in for a bad bout of malaria—cerebral type," he explained. " For that I proposed to treat myself by an intravenous injection of quinine. That is the usual method."

Poirot nodded his comprehension.

" The fever was on me badly. I fairly staggered into my tent. I could not at first find my case of drugs, someone had moved it from where I had originally placed it. Then, when I had found that, I could not find my hypodermic syringe. I hunted for it for some time, then gave it up and took a large dose of quinine by the mouth and flung myself on my bed."

Gerard paused, then went on:

" Mrs. Boynton's death was not discovered until after sunset. Owing to the way in which she was sitting and the support the chair gave to her body, no change occurred in her position and it was not until one of the boys went to summon her to dinner at six-thirty that it was noticed that anything was wrong."

He explained in full detail the position of the cave and its distance away from the big marquee.

" Miss King, who is a qualified doctor, examined the body. She did not disturb me, knowing that I had fever. There was, indeed, nothing that could be done. Mrs. Boynton was dead—and had been dead for some little time."

Poirot murmured: " How long exactly?"

Gerard said slowly:

" I do not think that Miss King gave much attention to that point. She did not, I presume, think it of any importance."

" One can say, at least, when she was last definitely known to be alive?" said Poirot.

Colonel Carbury cleared his throat and referred to an official-looking document.

" Mrs. Boynton was spoken to by Lady Westholme and Miss Pierce shortly after 4 p.m. Lennox Boynton spoke to his mother about four-thirty. Mrs. Lennox Boynton had a long conversation with her about five minutes later. Carol Boynton had a word with her mother at a time she is unable to state precisely—but which from the evidence of others would seem to have been about ten minutes past five.

"Jefferson Cope, an American friend of the family, returning to the camp with Lady Westholme and Miss Pierce, saw her asleep. He did not speak to her. That was about twenty to six. Raymond Boynton, the younger son, seems to have been the last person to see her alive. On his return from a walk he went and spoke to her at about ten minutes to six. The discovery of the body was made at six-thirty when a servant went to tell her dinner was ready."

"Between the time that Mr. Raymond Boynton spoke to her and half-past six did no one go near her?" asked Poirot.

"I understand not."

"But someone *might* have done so?" Poirot persisted.

"I don't think so. From close on six onwards servants were moving about the camp, people were going to and from their tents. No one can be found who saw anyone approaching the old lady."

"Then Raymond Boynton was definitely the last person to see his mother alive?" said Poirot.

Dr. Gerard and Colonel Carbury interchanged a quick glance. Colonel Carbury drummed on the table with his fingers.

"This is where we begin to get into deep waters," he said. "Go on, Gerard. This is your pigeon."

"As I mentioned just now, Sarah King, when she examined Mrs. Boynton, saw no reason for determining the exact time of death. She merely said that Mrs. Boynton had been dead 'some little time,' but when, on the following day for reasons of my own, I endeavoured to narrow things down and happened to mention that Mrs. Boynton was last seen alive by her son Raymond at a little before six, Miss King, to my great surprise, said point-blank that that was impossible—that at that time Mrs. Boynton must already have been dead."

Poirot's eyebrows rose. "Odd. Extremely odd. And what does M. Raymond Boynton say to that?"

Colonel Carbury said abruptly: "He swears that his mother was alive. He went up to her and said, "I'm back. Hope you have had a nice afternoon?' Something of that kind. He says she just grunted, 'Quite all right,' and he went on to his tent."

Poirot frowned perplexedly.

"Curious," he said. "Extremely curious. Tell me, was it growing dusk by then?"

"The sun was just setting."

"Curious," said Poirot again. "And you, Dr. Gerard, when did you see the body?"

"Not until the following day. At 9 a.m. to be precise."

"And your estimate of the time death had occurred?"

The Frenchman shrugged his shoulders.

"It is difficult to be exact after that length of time. There must necessarily be a margin of several hours. Were I giving evidence on oath I could only say that she had been dead certainly twelve hours and not longer than eighteen. You see, that does not help at all!"

"Go on, Gerard," said Colonel Carbury. "Give him the rest of it."

"On getting up in the morning," said Dr. Gerard, "I found my hypodermic syringe—it was behind a case of bottles on my dressing-table."

He leaned forward.

"You may say, if you like, that I had overlooked it the day before. I was in a miserable state of fever and wretchedness, shaking from head to foot, and how often does one look for a thing that is there all the time and yet be unable to find it! I can only say that I am quite positive the syringe was *not* there then."

"There's something more still," said Carbury.

"Yes, two facts for what they are worth and they mean a great deal. There was a mark on the dead woman's wrist—a mark such as would be caused by the insertion of a hypodermic syringe. Her daughter, I may say, explains it as having been caused by the prick of a pin——"

Poirot stirred. "Which daughter?"

"Her daughter Carol."

"Yes, continue, I pray you."

"And there is the last fact. Happening to examine my little case of drugs, I noticed that my stock of digitoxin was very much diminished."

"Digitoxin," said Poirot, "is a heart poison, is it not?"

"Yes. It is obtained from digitalis purpurea—the common foxglove. There are four active principles—*digitalin*—*digitonin*—*digitalein*—and *digitoxin*. Of these *digitoxin* is considered the most active poisonous constituent of digitalis

75

leaves. According to Kopp's experiments it is from six to ten times stronger than *digitalin* or *digitalein*. It is official in France—but not in the British Pharmacopœia."

" And a large dose of digitoxin?"

Dr. Gerard said gravely: " A large dose of digitoxin thrown suddenly on the circulation by intravenous injection would cause sudden death by quick palsy of the heart. It has been estimated that four mgrms. might prove fatal to an adult man."

" And Mrs. Boynton already suffered with heart trouble?"

" Yes, as a matter of fact she was actually taking a medicine containing digitalin."

"That," said Poirot, " is extremely interesting."

" D'you mean," asked Colonel Carbury, " that her death might have been attributed to an overdose of her own medicine?"

" That—yes. But I meant more than that."

" In some senses," said Dr. Gerard, " digitalin may be considered a cumulative drug. Moreover, as regards post-mortem appearance, the active principles of the digitalis may destroy life and leave no appreciative sign."

Poirot nodded slow appreciation.

" Yes, that is clever—very clever. Almost impossible to prove satisfactorily to a jury. Ah, but let me tell you, gentlemen, if this is a murder, it is a very clever murder! The hypodermic replaced, the poison employed, a poison which the victim was already taking—the possibilities of a mistake—or accident—are overwhelming. Oh, yes, there are brains here. There is thought—care—genius."

For a moment he sat in silence, then he raised his head. " And yet, one thing puzzles me."

" What is that?"

" The theft of the hypodermic syringe."

" It was taken," said Dr. Gerard quickly.

" Taken—and returned?"

" Yes."

" Odd," said Poirot. " Very odd. Otherwise everything fits so well. . . ."

Colonel Carbury looked at him curiously.

" Well?" he said. " What's your expert opinion? Was it murder—or wasn't it?"

Poirot held up a hand.

"One moment. We have not yet arrived at that point. There is still some evidence to consider."

"What evidence? You've had it all."

"Ah! but this is evidence *that I, Hercule Poirot*, bring to you."

He nodded his head and smiled a little at their two astonished faces.

"Yes, it is droll, that! That I, to whom you tell the story, should in return present you with a piece of evidence about which you do not know. It was like this. In the Solomon Hotel, one night, I go to the window to make sure it is closed——"

"Closed—or open?" asked Carbury.

"Closed," said Poirot firmly. "It was open, so naturally I go to close it. But before I do so, as my hand is on the latch, I hear a voice speaking—an agreeable voice, low and clear with a tremor in it of nervous excitement. I say to myself it is a voice I will know again. And what does it say, this voice? It says these words, ' *You do see, don't you, that she's got to be killed?* ' "

"At the moment, *naturellement*, I do not take those words as referring to a killing of flesh and blood. I think it is an author or perhaps a playwright who speaks. But now—*I am not so sure*. That is to say I am sure it was nothing of the kind."

Again he paused before saying: "Messieurs, I will tell you this—*to the best of my knowledge and belief* those words were spoken by a young man whom I saw later in the lounge of the hotel and who was, so they told me on inquiring, a young man of the name of Raymond Boynton."

Chapter 3

"RAYMOND BOYNTON said that!"

The exclamation broke from the Frenchman.

"You think it unlikely—psychologically speaking?" Poirot inquired placidly.

Gerard shook his head.

"No, I should not say that. I was surprised, yes. If you follow me, I was surprised just because Raymond Boynton was so eminently fitted to be a suspect."

77

Colonel Carbury sighed. "These psychological fellers!" the sigh seemed to say.

"Question is," he murmured, "what are we going to do about it?"

Gerard shrugged his shoulders.

"I do not see what you can do," he confessed. "The evidence is bound to be inconclusive. You may know that murder has been done but it will be difficult to prove it."

"I see," said Colonel Carbury. "We suspect that murder's been done and we just sit back and twiddle our fingers! Don't like it!" He added, as if in extenuation, his former odd plea, "I'm a tidy man."

"I know. I know." Poirot nodded his head sympathetically. "You would like to clear this up. You would like to know definitely exactly what occurred and how it occurred. And you, Dr. Gerard? You have said that there is nothing to be done—that the evidence is bound to be inconclusive? That is probably true. But are you satisfied that the matter should rest so?"

"She was a bad life," said Gerard slowly. "In any case, she might have died very shortly—a week—a month—a year."

"So you are satisfied?" persisted Poirot.

Gerard went on:

"There is no doubt that her death was—how shall we put it?—beneficial to the community. It has brought freedom to her family. They will have scope to develop—they are all, I think, people of good character and intelligence. They will be —now—useful members of society! The death of Mrs. Boynton, as I see it, has resulted in nothing but good."

Poirot repeated for the third time: "So you are satisfied?"

"No." Dr. Gerard pounded a fist suddenly on the table. "I am *not* ' satisfied,' as you put it! It is my instinct to preserve life—not to hasten death. Therefore, though my conscious mind may repeat that this woman's death was a good thing, my unconscious mind rebels against it! *It is not well, gentlemen, that a human being should die before her time has come.*"

Poirot smiled. He leaned back contented with the answer he had probed for so patiently.

Colonel Carbury said unemotionally: "He don't like murder! Quite right! No more do I."

He rose and poured himself out a stiff whisky and soda. His guests' glasses were still full.

"And now," he said, returning to the subject, "let's get down to brass tacks. *Is there anything to be done about it?* We don't like it—no! But we may have to lump it! No good making a fuss if you can't deliver the goods."

Gerard leaned forward. "What is your professional opinion, M. Poirot? You are the expert."

Poirot took a little time to speak. Methodically he arranged an ash-tray or two and made a little heap of used matches. Then he said:

"You desire to know, do you not, Colonel Carbury, *who killed Mrs. Boynton*? (That is if she *was* killed and did not die a natural death.) Exactly *how and when* she was killed—and in fact the whole truth of the matter?"

"I should like to know that, yes." Carbury spoke unemotionally.

Hercule Poirot said slowly: "I see no reason why you should not know it!"

Dr. Gerard looked incredulous. Colonel Carbury looked mildly interested.

"Oh," he said. "So you don't, don't you? That's interestin'. How d'you propose to set about it?"

"By methodical sifting of the evidence, by a process of reasoning."

"Suits me," said Colonel Carbury.

"And by a study of the psychological possibilities."

"Suits Dr. Gerard, I expect," said Carbury. "And after that—after you've sifted the evidence and done some reasoning and paddled in psychology—*hey presto!*—you think you can produce the rabbit out of the hat?"

"I should be extremely surprised if I could not do so," said Poirot calmly.

Colonel Carbury stared at him over the rim of his glass. Just for a moment the vague eyes were no longer vague—they measured—and appraised.

He put down his glass with a grunt.

"What do you say to that, Dr. Gerard?"

"I admit that I am sceptical of success. . . . Yes, I know that M. Poirot has great powers."

"I am gifted—yes," said the little man. He smiled modestly.

Colonel Carbury turned away his head and coughed.

Poirot said: "The first thing to decide is whether this is a composite murder—planned and carried out by the Boynton

79

family as a whole, or whether it is the work of one of them only. If the latter, which is the most likely member of the family to have attempted it."

Dr. Gerard said: " There is your own evidence. One must, I think, consider first Raymond Boynton."

" I agree," said Poirot. " The words I overheard and the discrepancy between his evidence and that of the young woman doctor puts him definitely in the forefront of the suspects.

" He was the last person to see Mrs. Boynton alive. That is his own story. Sarah King contradicts that. Tell me, Dr. Gerard, is there—eh?—you know what I mean—a little *tendresse*, shall we say—there?"

The Frenchman nodded. " Emphatically so."

" Aha! Is she, this young lady, a brunette with hair that goes back from her forehead—so—and big hazel eyes and a manner very decided?"

Dr. Gerard looked rather surprised.

" Yes, that describes her very well."

" I think I have seen her—in the Solomon Hotel. She spoke to this Raymond Boynton and afterwards he remained *planté là*—in a dream—blocking the exit from the lift. Three times I had to say ' Pardon ' before he heard me and moved."

He remained in thought for some moments. Then he said: " So, to begin with, we will accept the medical evidence of Miss Sarah King with certain mental reservations. She is an interested party." He paused—then went on: " Tell me, Dr. Gerard, do you think Raymond Boynton is of the temperament that could commit murder easily?"

Gerard said slowly: " You mean deliberate planned murder? Yes, I think it is possible—but only under conditions of intense emotional strain."

" Those conditions were present?"

" Definitely. This journey abroad undoubtedly heightened the nervous and mental strain under which all these people were living. The contrast between their own lives and those of other people was more apparent to them. And in Raymond Boynton's case——"

" Yes?"

" There was the additional complication of being strongly attracted to Sarah King."

" That would give him an additional motive? And an additional stimulus?"

"That is so."

Colonel Carbury coughed.

"Like to butt in a moment. That sentence of his you over-heard, 'You do see, don't you, that she's got to be killed?' Must have been spoken to someone."

"A good point," said Poirot. "I had not forgotten it. Yes, to whom was Raymond Boynton speaking? Undoubtedly to a member of his family. But which member? Can you tell us something, doctor, of the mental condition of the other members of the family?"

Gerard replied promptly:

"Carol Boynton was, I should say, in very much the same state as Raymond—a state of rebellion accompanied by a severe nervous excitement, but uncomplicated in her case by the introduction of a sex factor. Lennox Boynton had passed the stage of revolt. He was sunk in apathy. He was finding it, I think, difficult to concentrate. His method of reaction to his surroundings was to retire further and further within himself. He was definitely an introvert."

"And his wife?"

"His wife, though tired and unhappy, showed no signs of mental conflict. She was, I believe, hesitating on the brink of a decision."

"Such a decision being?"

"Whether or not to leave her husband."

He repeated the conversation he had held with Jefferson Cope. Poirot nodded in comprehension.

"And what of the younger girl—Ginevra her name is, is it not?"

The Frenchman's face was grave. He said:

"I should say that mentally she is in an extremely danger-ous condition. She has already begun to display symptoms of schizophrenia. Unable to bear the suppression of her life, she is escaping into a realm of fantasy. She has advanced delusions of persecution—that is to say, she claims to be a Royal Personage—in danger—enemies surrounding her—all the usual things!"

"And that—is dangerous?"

"Very dangerous. It is the beginning of what is often homi-cidal mania. The sufferer kills—not for the lust of killing—but in self-defence. He or she kills in order not to be killed them-selves. From their point of view it is eminently rational."

81

" So you think that Ginevra Boynton might have killed her mother?"

" Yes. But I doubt if she would have had the knowledge or the constructiveness to do it the way it was done. The cunning of that class of mania is usually very simple and obvious. And I am almost certain she would have chosen a more spectacular method."

" But she is a *possibility*?" Poirot insisted.

" Yes," admitted Gerard.

" And afterwards—when the deed was done? *Do you think the rest of the family knew who had done it?*"

" They know!" said Colonel Carbury unexpectedly. " If ever I came across a bunch of people who had something to hide—these are they! They're putting something over all right."

" We will make them tell us what it is," said Poirot.

" Third degree?" said Colonel Carbury.

" No." Poirot shook his head. " Just ordinary conversation. On the whole, you know, people tell you the truth. Because it is easier! Because it is less strain on the inventive faculties! You can tell one lie—or two lies—or three lies—or even four lies—*but you cannot lie all the time*. And so—the truth becomes plain."

" Something in that," agreed Carbury.

Then he said bluntly: " You'll talk to them, you say? That means you're willing to take this on."

Poirot bowed his head.

" Let us be very clear about this," he said. " What you demand, and what I undertake to supply, is the truth. But mark this, even when we have got the truth, there may be no *proof*. That is to say, no proof that would be accepted in a court of law. You comprehend?"

" Quite," said Carbury. " You satisfy me of what really happened. Then it's up to me to decide whether action is possible or not—having regard to the international aspects. Anyway, it will be cleared up—no mess. Don't like mess."

Poirot smiled.

" One thing more," said Carbury. " I can't give you much time. Can't detain these people here indefinitely."

Poirot said quietly:

" You can detain them twenty-four hours. You shall have the truth by to-morrow night."

Colonel Carbury stared hard at him.

" Pretty confident, aren't you?" he asked.

" I know my own ability," murmured Poirot.

Rendered uncomfortable by this un-British attitude, Colonel Carbury looked away and fingered his untidy moustache.

" Well," he mumbled, " it's up to you."

" And if you succeed, my friend," said Dr. Gerard, " you are indeed a marvel!"

Chapter 4

SARAH KING looked long and searchingly at Hercule Poirot. She noted the egg-shaped head, the gigantic moustaches, the dandyfied appearance and the suspicious blackness of his hair. A look of doubt crept into her eyes. " Well, mademoiselle, are you satisfied?"

Sarah flushed as she met the amused ironical glance of his eyes.

" I beg your pardon," she said awkwardly.

" Du tout! To use an expression I have recently learnt, you give me the once-over, is it not so?"

Sarah smiled a little. " Well, at any rate, you can do the same to me," she said.

" Assuredly. I have not neglected to do so."

She glanced at him sharply. Something in his tone. But Poirot was twirling his moustaches complacently, and Sarah thought (for the second time), " The man's a mountebank!"

Her self-confidence restored, she sat up a little straighter and said inquiringly: " I don't think I quite understand the object of this interview?"

" The good Dr. Gerard did not explain?"

Sarah said frowning: " I don't understand Dr. Gerard. He seems to think——"

" Something is rotten in the state of Denmark," quoted Poirot. " You see, I know your Shakespeare ."

Sarah waved aside Shakespeare.

" What exactly is all this fuss about?" she demanded.

" Eh bien, one wants, does one not, to get at the truth of this affair?"

" Are you talking about Mrs. Boynton's death?"

" Yes."

"Isn't it rather a fuss about nothing? You, of course, are a specialist, M. Poirot. It is natural for you——"

Poirot finished the sentence for her.

"It is natural for me to suspect crime whenever I can possibly find an excuse for doing so?"

"Well—yes—perhaps."

"You have no doubt yourself as to Mrs. Boynton's death?"

Sarah shrugged her shoulders.

"Really, M. Poirot, if you had been to Petra you would realise that the journey there was a somewhat strenuous business for an old woman whose cardiac condition was unsatisfactory."

"It seems a perfectly straightforward business to you?"

"Certainly. I can't understand Dr. Gerard's attitude. He didn't even know anything about it. He was down with fever. I'd bow to his superior medical knowledge naturally—in this case he had nothing whatever to go on. I suppose they can have a P.M. in Jerusalem if they like—if they're not satisfied with my verdict."

Poirot was silent for a moment, then he said:

"There is a fact, Miss King, that you do not yet know. Dr. Gerard has not told you of it."

"What fact?" demanded Sarah.

"A supply of a drug—digitoxin—is missing from Dr. Gerard's travelling medicine case."

"Oh!" Quickly Sarah took in this new aspect of the case. Equally quickly she pounced on the one doubtful point.

"Is Dr. Gerard quite sure of that?"

Poirot shrugged his shoulders.

"A doctor, as you should know, mademoiselle, is usually fairly careful in making his statements."

"Oh, of course. That goes without saying. But Dr. Gerard had malaria at the time."

"That is so, of course."

"Has he any idea when it could have been taken?"

"He had occasion to go to his case on the night of his arrival in Petra. He wanted some phenacetin—as his head was aching badly. When he replaced the phenacetin the following morning and shut up the case he is almost certain that all the drugs were intact."

"Almost——" said Sarah.

Poirot shrugged.

84

"Yes, there is a doubt! There is the doubt that any man, who is honest, would be likely to feel."

Sarah nodded. "Yes, I know. One always distrusts those people who are *over* sure. But all the same, M. Poirot, the evidence *is* very slight. It seems to me——" She paused. Poirot finished the sentence for her.

"It seems to you that an inquiry on my part is ill-advised!" Sarah looked him squarely in the face.

"Frankly, it does. Are you sure, M. Poirot, that this is not a case of Roman Holiday?"

Poirot smiled. "The private lives of a family upset and disturbed—so that Hercule Poirot can play a little game of detection to amuse himself?"

"I didn't mean to be offensive—but isn't it a little like that?"

"You, then, are on the side of the Famille Boynton, mademoiselle?"

"I think I am. They've suffered a good deal. They—they oughtn't to have to stand any more."

"And *la maman*, she was unpleasant, tyrannical, disagreeable and decidedly better dead than alive? That also—*hein*?"

"When you put it like that——" Sarah paused, flushed, went on: "One shouldn't, I agree, take that into consideration."

"But all the same—one does! That is, *you* do, mademoiselle! I—do not! To me it is all the same. The victim may be one of the good God's saints—or, on the contrary—a monster of infamy. It moves me not. The fact is the same. A life—taken! I say it always—I do not approve of murder."

"Murder?" Sarah drew in her breath sharply. "But what evidence of that is there? The flimsiest imaginable! Dr. Gerard himself cannot be sure!"

Poirot said quietly: "But there is other evidence, mademoiselle."

"What evidence?" Her voice was sharp.

"*The mark of a hypodermic puncture upon the dead woman's wrist.* And something more still—*some words that I overheard spoken in Jerusalem* on a clear, still night when I went to close my bedroom window. Shall I tell you what those words were, Miss King? They were these. I heard Mr. Raymond Boynton say: '*You do see, don't you, that she's got to be killed?*'"

He saw the colour drain slowly from Sarah's face.

She said: "*You heard that?*"

"Yes."

The girl stared straight ahead of her.

She said at last: "It would be you who heard it!"

He acquiesced.

"Yes, it would be me. These things happen. You see now why I think there should be an investigation?"

Sarah said quietly: "I think you are quite right."

"Ah! And you will help me?"

"Certainly."

Her tone was matter-of-fact—unemotional. Her eyes met his coolly.

Poirot bowed. "Thank you, mademoiselle. Now I will ask you to tell me in your own words exactly what you can remember of that particular day."

Sarah considered for a moment.

"Let me see. I went on an expedition in the morning. None of the Boyntons were with us. I saw them at lunch. They were finishing as we came in. Mrs. Boynton seemed in an unusually good temper."

"She was not usually amiable, I understand."

"Very far from it," said Sarah with a slight grimace.

She then described how Mrs. Boynton had released her family from attendance on her.

"That too, was unusual?"

"Yes. She usually kept them around her."

"Do you think, perhaps, that she suddenly felt remorseful —that she had what is called—*un bon moment*?"

"No, I don't," said Sarah bluntly.

"What did you think, then?"

"I was puzzled. I suspected it was something of the cat-and-mouse order."

"If you would elaborate, mademoiselle?"

"A cat enjoys letting a mouse away—and then catching it again. Mrs. Boynton had that kind of mentality. I thought she was up to some new devilry or other."

"What happened next, mademoiselle?"

"The Boyntons started off——"

"All of them?"

"No, the youngest, Ginevra, was left behind. She was told to go and rest."

"Did she wish to do so?"

" No. But that didn't matter. She did what she was told.
The others started off. Dr. Gerard and I joined them——"

" When was this?"

" About half-past three."

" Where was Mrs. Boynton then?"

" Nadine—young Mrs. Boynton—had settled her in her
chair outside her cave."

" Proceed."

" When we got round the bend, Dr. Gerard and I caught up
the others. We all walked together. Then, after a while, Dr.
Gerard turned back. He had been looking rather queer for
some time. I could see he had fever. I wanted to go back with
him, but he wouldn't hear of it."

" What time was this?"

" Oh! about four, I suppose."

" And the rest?"

" We went on."

" Were you all together?"

" At first. Then we split up." Sarah hurried on as though
foreseeing the next question. " Nadine Boynton and Mr.
Cope went one way and Carol, Lennox, Raymond and I went
another."

" And you continued like that?"

" Well—no. Raymond Boynton and I separated from the
others. We sat down on a slab of rock and admired the wild-
ness of the scenery. Then he went off and I stayed where I
was for some time longer. It was about half-past five when I
looked at my watch and realised I had better get back. I
reached the camp at six o'clock. It was just about sunset."

" You passed Mrs. Boynton on the way?"

" I noticed she was still in her chair up on the ridge."

" That did not strike you as odd—that she had not
moved?"

" No, because I had seen her sitting there the night before
when we arrived."

" I see. *Continuez.*"

" I went into the marquee. The others were all there—
except Dr. Gerard. I washed and then came back. They
brought in dinner and one of the servants went to tell Mrs.
Boynton. He came running back to say she was ill. I hurried
out. She was sitting in her chair just as she had been, but
as soon as I touched her I realised she was dead."

" You had no doubt at all as to her death being natural?"

87

"None whatever. I had heard that she suffered from heart trouble, though no specified disease had been mentioned."

"You simply thought she had died sitting there in her chair?"

"Yes."

"Without calling out for assistance?"

"Yes. It happens that way sometimes. She might even have died in her sleep. She was quite likely to have dozed off. In any case, all the camp was asleep most of the afternoon. No one would have heard her unless she had called very loud."

"Did you form an opinion as to how long she had been dead?"

"Well, I didn't really think very much about it. She had clearly been dead some time."

"What do you call some time?" asked Poirot.

"Well—over an hour. It might have been much longer. The refraction of the rock would keep her body from cooling quickly."

"Over an hour? Are you aware, Mademoiselle King, that Mr. Raymond Boynton spoke to her only a little over half an hour earlier, and that she was then alive and well?"

Now her eyes no longer met his. But she shook her head. "He must have made a mistake. It must have been earlier than that."

"No, mademoiselle, it was not."

She looked at him point-blank. He noticed again the firm set of her mouth.

"Well," said Sarah, "I'm young and I haven't got much experience of dead bodies—but I know enough to be quite sure of one thing. Mrs. Boynton had been dead *at least* an hour when I examined her body!"

"That," said Hercule Poirot unexpectedly, "is your story and you are going to stick to it! Then can you explain *why* Mr. Boynton should say his mother was alive when she was, in point of fact, dead?"

"I've no idea," said Sarah. "They're probably rather vague about times, all of them! They're a very nervy family."

"On how many occasions, mademoiselle, have you spoken with them?"

Sarah was silent a moment, frowning a little.

"I can tell you exactly," she said. "I talked to Raymond Boynton in the Wagon Lits corridor coming to Jerusalem. I had two conversations with Carol Boynton—one at the Mosque of Omar and one late that evening in my bedroom. I had a conversation with Mrs. Lennox Boynton the following morning. That's all—up to the afternoon of Mrs. Boynton's death, when we all went walking together."

"You did not have any conversation with Mrs. Boynton herself?"

Sarah flushed uncomfortably.

"Yes. I exchanged a few words with her the day she left Jerusalem." She paused and then blurted out: "As a matter of fact, I made a fool of myself."

"Ah?"

The interrogation was so patent that, stiffly and unwillingly, Sarah gave an account of the conversation.

Poirot seemed interested and cross-examined her closely.

"The mentality of Mrs. Boynton—it is very important in this case," he said. "And you are an outsider—an unbiased observer. That is why your account of her is very significant."

Sarah did not reply. She still felt hot and uncomfortable when she thought of that interview.

"Thank you, mademoiselle," said Poirot. "I will now converse with the other witnesses."

Sarah rose. "Excuse me, M. Poirot, but if I might make a suggestion——"

"Certainly. Certainly."

"Why not postpone all this until an autopsy can be made and you discover whether or not your suspicions are justified? I think all this is rather like putting the cart before the horse."

Poirot waved a grandiloquent hand. "This is the method of Hercule Poirot," he announced.

Pressing her lips together, Sarah left the room.

Chapter 5

LADY WESTHOLME entered the room with the assurance of a transatlantic liner coming into dock.

Miss Amabel Pierce, an indeterminate craft, followed in the liner's wake and sat down in an inferior make of chair slightly in the background.

"Certainly, M. Poirot," boomed Lady Westholme. "I shall

be delighted to assist you by any means in my power. I have always considered that in matters of this kind one has a public duty to perform——"

When Lady Westholme's public duty had held the stage for some minutes, Poirot was adroit enough to get in a question.

"I have a perfect recollection of the afternoon in question," replied Lady Westholme. "Miss Pierce and I will do all we can to assist you."

"Oh, yes," sighed Miss Pierce, almost ecstatically. "So tragic, was it not? Dead—just like that—in the twinkle of an eye!"

"If you will tell me exactly what occurred on the afternoon in question?"

"Certainly," said Lady Westholme. "After we had finished lunch I decided to take a brief siesta. The morning excursion had been somewhat fatiguing. Not that I was really tired—I seldom am. I do not really know what fatigue is. One has so often, on public occasions, no matter what one really feels——"

Again an adroit murmur from Poirot.

"As I say, I was in favour of a siesta. Miss Pierce agreed with me."

"Oh, yes," sighed Miss Pierce. "And I was *terribly* tired after the morning. Such a *dangerous* climb—and although interesting, *most* exhausting. I'm afraid I'm not *quite* as strong as Lady Westholme."

"Fatigue," said Lady Westholme, "can be conquered like everything else. I make a point of never giving in to my bodily needs."

Poirot said:

"After lunch, then, you two ladies went to your tents?"

"Yes."

"Mrs. Boynton was then sitting at the mouth of her cave?"

"Her daughter-in-law assisted her there before she herself went off."

"You could both see her?"

"Oh, yes," said Miss Pierce. "She was opposite, you know —only, of course, a little way along and up above."

Lady Westholme elucidated the statement.

"The caves opened on to a ledge. Below that ledge were some tents. Then there was a small stream and across that stream was the big marquee and some other tents. Miss Pierce and I had tents near the marquee. She was on the right side of the marquee and I was on the left. The opening of our tents faced the ledge, but of course it was some distance away."

"Nearly two hundred yards, I understand."

"Possibly."

"I have here a plan," said Poirot, "concocted with the help of the dragoman, Mahmoud."

Lady Westholme remarked that in that case it was probably wrong!

"That man is grossly inaccurate. I have checked his statements from my Baedeker. Several times his information was definitely misleading."

"According to my plan, said Poirot, "the cave next to Mrs. Boynton's was occupied by her son, Lennox, and his wife. Raymond, Carol and Ginevra Boynton had tents just below but more to the right—in fact, almost opposite the marquee. On the right of Ginevra Boynton's was Dr. Gerard's tent and next to that again that of Miss King. On the other side of the stream—next to the marquee on the left—you and Mr. Cope had tents. Miss Pierce's, as you mentioned, was on the right of the marquee. Is that correct?"

Lady Westholme admitted grudgingly that as far as she knew it was.

"I thank you. That is perfectly clear. Pray continue, Lady Westholme."

Lady Westholme smiled graciously on him and went on:

"At about quarter to four I strolled along to Miss Pierce's tent to see if she were awake yet and felt like a stroll. She was sitting in the doorway of the tent reading. We agreed to start in about half an hour when the sun was less hot. I went back to my tent and read for about twenty-five minutes. Then I went along and joined Miss Pierce. She was ready and we started out. Everyone in the camp seemed asleep—there was no one about, and seeing Mrs. Boynton sitting up there alone, I suggested to Miss Pierce that we should ask her if she wanted anything before we left."

"Yes, you did. *Most* thoughtful of you, I considered," murmured Miss Pierce.

"I felt it to be my duty," said Lady Westholme with a rich complacency.

"And then for her to be so rude about it!" exclaimed Miss Pierce.

Poirot looked inquiring.

"Our path passed just under the ledge," explained Lady

Westholme, "and I called up to her, saying that we were going for a stroll and could we do anything for her before we went. Do you know, M. Poirot, absolutely the only answer she gave us was a *grunt*! A grunt! She just looked at us as though we were—as though we were dirt!"

"Disgraceful it was!" said Miss Pierce, flushing.

"I must confess," said Lady Westholme, reddening a little, "that I made then a somewhat uncharitable remark."

"I think you were quite justified," said Miss Pierce. "*Quite*—under the circumstances."

"What was this remark?" asked Poirot.

"I said to Miss Pierce that perhaps she *drank*! Really her manner was *most* peculiar. It had been all along. I thought it possible that drink might account for it. The evils of alcoholic indulgence, as I very well know——"

Dexterously, Poirot steered the conversation away from the drink question.

"Had her manner been very peculiar on this particular day? At lunch-time, for instance?"

"N-No," said Lady Westholme, considering. "No, I should say then that her manner had been fairly normal—for an American of that type, that is to say," she added condescendingly.

"She was very abusive to that servant," said Miss Pierce.

"Which one?"

"Not very long before we started out."

"Oh! yes, I remember, she *did* seem extraordinarily annoyed with him! Of course," went on Lady Westholme, "to have servants about who cannot understand a word of English is very trying, but what I say is that when one is travelling one must make allowances."

"What servant was this?" asked Poirot.

"One of the Bedouin servants attached to the camp. He went up to her—I think she must have sent him to fetch her something, and I suppose he brought the wrong thing—I don't really know what it was—but she was very angry about it. The poor man slunk away as fast as he could, and she shook her stick at him and called out."

"What did she call out?"

"We were too far away to hear. At least I didn't hear anything distinctly, did you, Miss Pierce?"

"No, I didn't. I think she'd sent him to fetch something from her youngest daughter's tent—or perhaps she was angry with him for going into her daughter's tent—I couldn't say exactly."

" What did he look like?"

Miss Pierce, to whom the question was addressed, shook her head vaguely.

" Really, I couldn't say. He was too far away. All these Arabs look alike to me."

" He was a man of more than average height," said Lady Westholme, " and wore the usual native head-dress. He had on a pair of very torn and patched breeches—really disgraceful they were—and his puttees were wound most untidily—all anyhow! These men need *discipline*!"

" You could point the man out among the camp servants?"

" I doubt it. We didn't see his face—it was too far away. And, as Miss Pierce says, really these Arabs look all alike."

" I wonder," said Poirot thoughtfully, " what it was he did to make Mrs. Boynton so angry?"

" They are very trying to the patience sometimes," said Lady Westholme. " One of them took my shoes away, though I had expressly told him—by pantomime too— that I preferred to clean my shoes myself."

" Always I do that, too," said Poirot, diverted for a moment from his interrogation. " I take everywhere my little shoe-cleaning outfit. Also, I take a duster."

" So do I." Lady Westholme sounded quite human.

" Because these Arabs they do not remove the dust from one's belongings——"

" Never! Of course one has to dust one's things three or four times a day——"

" But it is well worth it."

" Yes, indeed. I cannot STAND dirt!"

Lady Westholme looked positively militant.

She added with feeling:

" The flies—in the bazaars—terrible!"

" Well, well," said Poirot, looking slightly guilty. " We can soon inquire from this man what it was that irritated Mrs. Boynton. To continue with your story?"

" We strolled along slowly," said Lady Westholme. " And then we met Dr. Gerard. He was staggering along and looked very ill. I could see at once he had fever."

" He was shaking," put in Miss Pierce. " Shaking all over."

" I saw at once he had an attack of malaria coming on," said Lady Westholme. " I offered to come back with him and get him some quinine, but he said he had his own supply with him."

"Poor man," said Miss Pierce. "You know it always seems so dreadful to me to see a doctor ill. It seems all wrong somehow."

"We strolled on," continued Lady Westholme. "And then we sat down on a rock."

Miss Pierce murmured: "Really—so tired after the morning's exertion—the climbing——"

"I never feel fatigue," said Lady Westholme firmly. "But there was no point in going farther. We had a very good view of all the surrounding scenery."

"Were you out of sight of the camp?"

"No, we were sitting facing towards it."

"So romantic," murmured Miss Pierce. "A camp pitched in the middle of a wilderness of rose-red rocks."

She sighed and shook her head.

"That camp could be much better run than it is," said Lady Westholme. Her rocking-horse nostrils dilated. "I shall take up the matter with Castle's. I am not at all sure that the drinking water is boiled as well as filtered. It should be. I shall point that out to them."

Poirot coughed and led the conversation quickly away from the subject of drinking water.

"Did you see any other members of the party?" he inquired.

"Yes. The elder Mr. Boynton and his wife passed us on their way back to the camp."

"Were they together?"

"No, Mr. Boynton came first. He looked a little as though he had had a touch of the sun. He was walking as though he were slightly dizzy."

"The back of the neck," said Miss Pierce. "One *must* protect the back of the neck! I always wear a thick silk handkerchief."

"What did Mr. Lennox Boynton do on his return to the camp?" asked Poirot.

For once Miss Pierce managed to get in first before Lady Westholme could speak.

"He went right up to his mother, but he didn't stay long with her."

"How long?"

"Just a minute or two."

94

" I should put it at just over a minute myself," said Lady Westholme. " Then he went on into his cave and after that he went down to the marquee."

" And his wife?"

" She came along about a quarter of an hour later. She stopped a minute and spoke to us—quite civilly."

" I think she's very nice," said Miss Pierce. " Very nice indeed."

" She is not so impossible as the rest of the family," allowed Lady Westholme.

" You watched her return to the camp?"

" Yes. She went up and spoke to her mother-in-law. Then she went into her cave and brought out a chair, and sat by her talking for some time—about ten minutes, I should say."

" And then?"

" Then she took the chair back to the cave and went down to the marquee where her husband was."

" What happened next?"

" That very peculiar American came along," said Lady Westholme. " Cope, I think his name is. He told us that there was a very good example of the debased architecture of the period just round the bend of the valley. He said we ought not to miss it. Accordingly, we walked there. Mr. Cope had with him quite an interesting article on Petra and the Nabateans."

" It was all *most* interesting," declared Miss Pierce.

Lady Westholme continued:

" We strolled back to the camp, it being then about twenty minutes to six. It was growing quite chilly."

" Mrs. Boynton was still sitting where you had left her?"

" Yes."

" Did you speak to her?"

" No. As a matter of fact I hardly noticed her."

" What did you do next?"

" I went to my tent, changed my shoes and got out my own packet of China tea. I then went to the marquee. The dragoman was there and I directed him to make some tea for Miss Pierce and myself with the tea I had brought and to make quite sure that the water with which it was made was boiling. He said that dinner would be ready in about half an hour—the boys were laying the table at the time—but I said that made no difference."

" *I* always say a cup of tea makes *all* the difference," murmured Miss Pierce vaguely.

" Was there anyone in the marquee?"

" Oh, yes. Mr. and Mrs. Lennox Boynton were sitting at one end reading. And Carol Boynton was there too."

" And Mr. Cope?"

" He joined us at our tea," said Miss Pierce. " Though he said tea drinking wasn't an American habit."

Lady Westholme coughed.

" I became just a little afraid that Mr. Cope was going to be a nuisance—that he might fasten himself upon me. It is a little difficult sometimes to keep people at arm's length when one is travelling. I find they are inclined to presume. Americans, especially, are sometimes rather dense."

Poirot murmured suavely:

" I am sure, Lady Westholme, that you are quite capable of dealing with situations of that kind. When travelling acquaintances are no longer of any use to you, I am sure you are an adept at dropping them."

" I think I am capable of dealing with most situations," said Lady Westholme complacently.

The twinkle in Poirot's eye was quite lost upon her.

" If you will just conclude your recital of the day's happenings?" murmured Poirot.

" Certainly. As far as I can remember, Raymond Boynton and the red-haired Boynton girl came in shortly afterwards. Miss King arrived last. Dinner was then ready to be served. One of the servants was dispatched by the dragoman to announce the fact to old Mrs. Boynton. The man came running back with one of his comrades in a state of some agitation and spoke to the dragoman in Arabic. There was some mention of Mrs. Boynton being taken ill. Miss King offered her services. She went out with the dragoman. She came back and broke the news to the members of Mrs. Boynton's family."

" She did it very abruptly," put in Miss Pierce. " Just blurted it out. I think myself it ought to have been done more gradually."

" And how did Mrs. Boynton's family take the news?" asked Poirot.

For once both Lady Westholme and Miss Pierce seemed a little at a loss. The former said at last in a voice lacking its usual self-assurance:

"Well—really—it is difficult to say. They—they were very quiet about it."

"Stunned," said Miss Pierce.

She offered the word more as a suggestion than as a fact.

"They all went out with Miss King," said Lady Westholme. "Miss Pierce and I very sensibly remained where we were."

A faintly wistful look was observable in Miss Pierce's eye at this point.

"I detest vulgar curiosity!" continued Lady Westholme.

The wistful look became more pronounced. It was clear that Miss Pierce had had perforce to hate vulgar curiosity, too!

"Later," concluded Lady Westholme, "the dragoman and Miss King returned. I suggested that dinner should be served immediately to the four of us, so that the Boynton family could dine later in the marquee without the embarrassment of strangers being present. My suggestion was adopted and immediately after the meal I retired to my tent. Miss King and Miss Pierce did the same. Mr. Cope, I believe, remained in the marquee as he was a friend of the family and thought he might be of some assistance to them. That is all I know, M. Poirot."

"When Miss King had broken the news, *all* the Boynton family accompanied her out of the marquee?"

"Yes—no, I believe, now that you come to mention it, that the red-haired girl stayed behind. Perhaps you can remember, Miss Pierce?"

"Yes, I think—I am quite sure she did."

Poirot asked: "What did she do?"

Lady Westholme stared at him.

"What did she *do*, M. Poirot? She did not do anything as far as I can remember."

"I mean was she sewing—or reading—did she look anxious—did she say anything?"

"Well, really——" Lady Westholme frowned. "She—er—she just sat there as far as I can remember."

"She twiddled her fingers," said Miss Pierce suddenly, "I remember noticing—poor thing, I thought, it shows what she's feeling! Not that there was anything to show in her *face,* you know—just her hands turning and twisting."

"Once," went on Miss Pierce conversationally, "I remember tearing up a pound note that way—not thinking of what I was doing. 'Shall I catch the first train and go to her?' I thought (it was a great-aunt of mine—taken suddenly ill). ' Or shall I *not*?' And I couldn't make up my mind one way or the other and there, I looked down, and instead of the telegram I was tearing up a pound note—*a pound note*—into tiny pieces!"

Miss Pierce paused dramatically.

Not entirely approving of this sudden bid for the limelight on the part of her satellite, Lady Westholme said coldly: " Is there anything else, M. Poirot?"

With a start, Poirot seemed to come out of a brown study. " Nothing—nothing—you have been most clear—most definite."

" I have an excellent memory," said Lady Westholme with satisfaction.

" One last little demand, Lady Westholme," said Poirot. " Please continue to sit as you are sitting—without looking round. Now would you be so kind as to describe to me just what Miss Pierce is wearing to-day—that is if Miss Pierce does not object?"

" Oh, no! not in the least!" twittered Miss Pierce.

" Really, M. Poirot, is there any *object*——"

" Please be so kind as to do as I ask, madame."

Lady Westholme shrugged her shoulders and then said with a rather bad grace:

" Miss Pierce has on a striped brown and white cotton dress, and is wearing with it a Sudanese belt of red, blue and biege leather. She is wearing beige silk stockings and brown *glacé* strap shoes. There is a ladder in her left stocking. She has a necklace of cornelian beads and one of bright royal blue beads —and is wearing a brooch with a pearl butterfly on it. She has an imitation scarab ring on the third finger of her right hand. On her head she has a double terai of pink and brown felt."

She paused—a pause of quiet competence. Then:

" Is there anything further?" she asked coldly.

Poirot spread out his hands in a wild gesture.

" You have my entire admiration, madame. Your observation is of the highest order."

" Details rarely escape me."

Lady Westholme rose, made a slight inclination of her head, and left the room. As Miss Pierce was following her, gazing down ruefully at her left leg, Poirot said:

" A little moment, please, mademoiselle?"

"Yes?" Miss Pierce looked up, a slightly apprehensive look upon her face.

Poirot leaned forward confidentially.

"You see this bunch of wild flowers on the table here?"

"Yes," said Miss Pierce—staring.

"And you noticed that when you first came into the room I sneezed once or twice?"

"Yes?"

"Did you notice if I had just been sniffing those flowers?"

"Well—really—no—I couldn't say."

"But you remember my sneezing?"

"Oh yes, I remember *that*!"

Ah, well—no matter. I wondered, you see, if these flowers might induce the hay fever. No matter!"

"Hay fever?" cried Miss Pierce. "I remember a cousin of mine was a *martyr* to it! She always said that if you sprayed your nose daily with a solution of boracic——"

With some difficulty Poirot shelved the cousin's nasal treatment and got rid of Miss Pierce. He shut the door and came back into the room with his eyebrows raised.

"But I did not sneeze," he murmured. "So much for that. No, I did not sneeze."

Chapter 6

LENNOX BOYNTON came into the room with a quick, resolute step. Had he been there, Dr. Gerard would have been surprised at the change in the man. The apathy was gone. His bearing was alert—although he was plainly nervous. His eyes had a tendency to shift rapidy from point to point about the room.

"Good morning, M. Boynton." Poirot rose and bowed ceremoniously. Lennox responded somewhat awkwardly. "I much appreciate your giving me this interview."

Lennox Boynton said rather uncertainly: "Er—Colonel Carbury said it would be a good thing—advised it—some formalities—he said."

"Please sit down, M. Boynton."

Lennox sat down on the chair lately vacated by Lady Westholme. Poirot went on conversationally:

"This has been a great shock to you, I am afraid?"

99

"Yes, of course. Well, no, perhaps not. . . . We always knew that my mother's heart was not strong."

"Was it wise, under those circumstances, to allow her to undertake such an arduous expedition?"

Lennox Boynton raised his head. He spoke not without a certain sad dignity.

"My mother, M.—er—Poirot, made her own decisions. If she made up her mind to anything it was no good our opposing her."

He drew in his breath sharply as he said the last words. His face suddenly went rather white.

"I know well," admitted Poirot, "that elderly ladies are sometimes headstrong."

Lennox said irritably:

"What is the purpose of all this? That is what I want to know. Why have all these formalities arisen?"

"Perhaps you do not realise, Mr. Boynton, that in cases of sudden and unexplained deaths, formalities must necessarily arise."

Lennox said sharply: "What do you mean by 'unexplained'?"

Poirot shrugged his shoulders.

"There is always the question to be considered: Is a death natural—or might it perhaps be suicide?"

"Suicide?" Lennox Boynton stared.

Poirot said lightly:

"You, of course, would know best about such possibilities. Colonel Carbury, naturally, is in the dark. It is necessary for him to decide whether to order an inquiry—an autopsy—all the rest of it. As I was on the spot and as I have much experience of these matters, he suggested that I should make a few inquiries and advise him upon the matter. Naturally he does not wish to cause you inconvenience if it can be helped."

Lennox Boynton said angrily: "I shall wire to our Consul in Jerusalem."

Poirot said non-committally: "You are quite within your rights in doing so, of course."

There was a pause. Then Poirot said, spreading out his hands:

"If you object to answering my questions——"

Lennox Boynton said quickly: "Not at all. Only—it seems—all so unnecessary."

"I comprehend. I comprehend perfectly. But it is all very

100

simple, really. A matter, as they say, of routine. Now, on the afternoon of your mother's death, M. Boynton, I believe you left the camp at Petra and went for a walk?"

"Yes. We all went—with the exception of my mother and my youngest sister."

"Your mother was then sitting in the mouth of her cave?"

"Yes, just outside it. She sat there every afternoon."

"Quite so. You started—when?"

"Soon after three, I should say."

"You returned from your walk—when?"

"I really couldn't say what time it was—four o'clock, five o'clock perhaps."

"About an hour to two hours after you set out?"

"Yes—about that, I should think."

"Did you pass anyone on your way back?"

"Did I what?"

"Pass anyone. Two ladies sitting on a rock, for instance."

"I don't know. Yes, I think I did."

"You were, perhaps, too absorbed in your thoughts to notice?"

"Yes, I was."

"Did you speak to your mother when you got back to the camp?"

"Yes—yes, I did."

"She did not then complain of feeling ill?"

"No—no, she seemed perfectly all right."

"May I ask what exactly passed between you?"

Lennox paused a minute.

"She said I had come back soon. I said, yes, I had." He paused again in an effort of concentration. "I said it was hot. She—she asked me the time—said her wrist-watch had stopped. I took it from her, wound it up, set it, and put it back on her wrist."

Poirot interrupted gently: "And what time was it?"

"Eh?" said Lennox.

"What time was it when you set the hands of the wrist-watch?"

"Oh, I see. It—it was twenty-five minutes to five."

"So you do know exactly the time you returned to the camp!" said Poirot gently.

Lennox flushed.

"Yes, what a fool I am! I'm sorry, M. Poirot, my wits are all astray, I'm afraid. All this worry——"

Poirot chimed in quickly: "Oh! I understand—I understand perfectly! It is all of the most disquieting! And what happened next?"

"I asked my mother if she wanted anything. A drink—tea, coffee, etc. She said no. Then I went to the marquee. None of the servants seemed to be about, but I found some soda water and drank it. I was thirsty. I sat there reading some old numbers of the *Saturday Evening Post*. I think I must have dozed off."

"Your wife joined you in the marquee?"

"Yes, she came in not long after."

"And you did not see your mother again alive?"

"No."

"She did not seem in any way agitated or upset when you were talking to her?"

"No, she was exactly as usual."

"She did not refer to any trouble or annoyance with one of the servants?"

Lennox stared.

"No, nothing at all."

"And that is all you can tell me?"

"I am afraid so—yes."

"Thank you, Mr. Boynton."

Poirot inclined his head as a sign that the interview was over. Lennox did not seem very willing to depart. He stood hesitating by the door. "Er—there's nothing else?"

"Nothing. Perhaps you would be so good as to ask your wife to come here?"

Lennox went slowly out. On the pad beside him Poirot wrote L.B. 4.35 p.m.

Chapter 7

POIROT LOOKED with interest at the tall, dignified young woman who entered the room. He rose and bowed to her politely. "Mrs. Lennox Boynton? Hercule Poirot, at your service."

Nadine Boynton sat down. Her thoughtful eyes were on Poirot's face.

"I hope you do not mind, madame, my intruding on your sorrow in this way?"

102

Her eyes did not waver. She did not reply at once. Her eyes remained steady and grave. At last she gave a sigh and said: "I think it is best for me to be quite frank with you, M. Poirot."

"I agree with you, madame."

"You apologised for intruding upon my sorrow. That sorrow, M. Poirot, does not exist and it is idle to pretend that it does. I had no love for my mother-in-law and I cannot honestly say that I regret her death."

"Thank you, madame, for your plain speaking."

Nadine went on: "Still, although I cannot pretend sorrow, I can admit to another feeling—remorse."

"Remorse?" Poirot's eyebrows went up.

"Yes. Because, you see, it was I who brought about her death. For that I blame myself bitterly."

"What is this you are saying, madame?"

"I am saying that I was the cause of my mother-in-law's death. I was acting, as I thought, honestly—but the result was unfortunate. To all intents and purposes, I killed her."

Poirot leaned back in his chair. "Will you be so kind as to elucidate this statement, madame?"

Nadine bent her head.

"Yes, that is what I wish to do. My first reaction, naturally, was to keep my private affairs to myself, but I see that the time has come when it would be better to speak out. I have no doubt, M. Poirot, that you have often received confidences of a somewhat intimate nature?"

"That, yes."

"Then I will tell you quite simply what occurred. My married life, M. Poirot, has not been particularly happy. My husband is not entirely to blame for that—his mother's influence over him has been unfortunate—but I have been feeling for some time that my life was becoming intolerable."

She paused and then went on:

"On the afternoon of my mother-in-law's death I came to a decision. I have a friend—a very good friend. He has suggested more than once that I should throw in my lot with his. On that afternoon I accepted his proposal."

"You decided to leave your husband?"

"Yes."

"Continue, madame."

Nadine said in a lower voice:

"Having once made my decision, I wanted to—to establish

103

it as soon as possible. I walked home to the camp by myself. My mother-in-law was sitting alone, there was no one about, and I decided to break the news to her then and there. I got a chair—sat down by her and told her abruptly what I had decided."

"She was surprised?"

"Yes, I am afraid it was a great shock to her. She was both surprised and angry—very angry. She—she worked herself into quite a state about it! Presently I refused to discuss the matter any longer. I got up and walked away." Her voice dropped. "I—I never saw her again alive."

Poirot nodded his head slowly. He said: "I see."

Then he said: "You think her death was the result of the shock?"

"It seems to me almost certain. You see, she had already over-exerted herself considerably getting to this place. My news, and her anger at it, would do the rest. . . . I feel additionally guilty because I have had a certain amount of training in illness and so I, more than anyone else, ought to have realised the possibility of such a thing happening."

Poirot sat in silence for some minutes, then he said:

"What exactly did you do when you left her?"

"I took the chair I had brought out back into my cave, then I went down to the marquee. My husband was there."

Poirot watched her closely as he said:

"Did you tell *him* of your decision? Or had you already told him?"

There was a pause, an infinitesimal pause before Nadine said: "I told him then."

"How did he take it?"

She answered quietly: "He was very upset."

"Did he urge you to reconsider your decision?"

She shook her head.

"He—he didn't say very much. You see, we had both known for some time that something like this might happen."

Poirot said: "You will pardon me, but—the other man was, of course, Mr. Jefferson Cope?"

She bent her head. "Yes."

There was a long pause, then, without any change of voice, Poirot asked: "Do you own a hypodermic syringe, madame?"

"Yes—no."

His eyebrows rose.

She explained: " I have an old hypodermic amongst other things in a travelling medicine chest, but it is in our big luggage which we left in Jerusalem."

" I see."

There was a pause, then she said, with a shiver of uneasiness: " Why did you ask me that, M. Poirot?"

He did not answer the question. Instead he put one of his own. " Mrs. Boynton was, I believe, taking a mixture containing digitalis?"

" Yes."

He thought that she was definitely watchful now.

" That was for her heart trouble?"

" Yes."

" Digitalis is, to some extent, a cumulative drug?"

" I believe it is. I do not know very much about it."

" If Mrs. Boynton had taken a big overdose of digitalis——"

She interrupted him quickly but with decision.

" She did not. She was always most careful. So was I if I measured the dose for her."

" There might have been an overdose in this particular bottle. A mistake of the chemist who made it up?"

" I think that is very unlikely," she replied quietly.

" Ah, well: the analysis will soon tell us."

Nadine said: " Unfortunately the bottle was broken."

Poirot eyed her with sudden interest.

" Indeed. Who broke it?"

" I'm not quite sure. One of the servants, I think. In carrying my mother-in-law's body into her cave, there was a good deal of confusion and the light was very poor. A table got knocked over."

Poirot eyed her steadily for a minute or two.

" That," he said, " is very interesting."

Nadine Boynton shifted wearily in her chair.

" You are suggesting, I think, that my mother-in-law did not die of shock, but of an overdose of digitalis?" she said, and went on: " That seems to me most improbable."

Poirot leaned forward.

" *Even when I tell you that Dr. Gerard, the French physician who was staying in the camp, had missed an appreciable quantity of a preparation of digitoxin from his medicine chest?*"

Her face grew very pale. He saw the clutch of her hand on

the table. Her eyes dropped. She sat very still. She was like a Madonna carved in stone.

"Well, madame," said Poirot at last, "what have you to say to that?"

The seconds ticked on but she did not speak. It was quite two minutes before she raised her head, and he started a little when he saw the look in her eyes.

"M. Poirot, *I did not kill my mother-in-law*. That you know! She was alive and well when I left her. There are many people who can testify to that! Therefore, being innocent of the crime, I can venture to appeal to you. Why must you mix yourself up in this business? If I swear to you on my honour that justice and only justice has been done, will you not abandon this inquiry? There has been so much suffering —you do not know. Now that at last there is peace and the possibility of happiness, must you destroy it all?"

Poirot sat up very straight. His eyes shone with a green light. "Let me be clear, madame; what are you asking me to do?"

"I am telling you that my mother-in-law died a natural death and I am asking you to accept that statement."

"Let us be definite. *You believe that your mother-in-law was deliberately killed*, and you are asking me to condone murder!"

"I am asking you to have pity!"

"Yes—on someone who had no pity!"

"You don't understand—it was not like that."

"Did you commit the crime yourself, madame, that you know so well?"

Nadine shook her head. She showed no signs of guilt. "No," she said quietly. "She was alive when I left her."

"And then—what happened? You *know*—or you *suspect*?"

Nadine said passionately:

"I have heard, M. Poirot, that once, in that affair of the Orient Express, you accepted an official verdict of what had happened?"

Poirot looked at her curiously. "I wonder who told you that."

"Is it true?"

He said slowly: "That case was—different."

"No. No, it was not different! The man who was killed was evil "—her voice dropped—" as *she* was. . . ."

Poirot said: "The moral character of the victim has nothing to do with it! A human being who has exercised the right of private judgment and taken the life of another human being is not safe to exist amongst the community. *I* tell you that! I, Hercule Poirot!"

"How hard you are!"

"Madame, in some ways I am adamant. I will not condone murder! That is the final word of Hercule Poirot."

She got up. Her dark eyes flashed with sudden fire.

"Then go on! Bring ruin and misery into the lives of innocent people! I have nothing more to say."

"But I, I think, madame, that you have a lot to say. . . ."

"No, nothing more."

"But, yes. What happened, madame, *after* you left your mother-in-law? Whilst you and your husband were in the marquee together?"

She shrugged her shoulders. "How should I know?"

"You *do* know—or you suspect."

She looked him straight in the eyes. "I know nothing, M. Poirot."

Turning she left the room.

Chapter 8

AFTER NOTING on his pad—N.B. 4.40—Poirot opened the door and called to the orderly whom Colonel Carbury had left at his disposal, an intelligent man with a good knowledge of English. He asked him to fetch Miss Carol Boynton.

He looked with some interest at the girl as she entered, at the chestnut hair, the poise of the head on the long neck, the nervous energy of the beautifully shaped hands.

He said: "Sit down, mademoiselle."

She sat down obediently. Her face was colourless and expressionless. Poirot began with a mechanical expression of sympathy to which the girl acquiesced without any change of expression.

"And now, mademoiselle, will you recount to me how you spent the afternoon of the day in question?"

Her answer came promptly, raising the suspicion that it had already been well rehearsed.

" After luncheon we all went for a stroll. I returned to the camp——"

Poirot interrupted. " A little minute. Were you all together until then?"

" No, I was with my brother Raymond and Miss King for most of the time. Then I strolled off on my own."

" Thank you. And you were saying you returned to the camp. Do you know the approximate time?"

" I believe it was just about ten minutes past five."

Poirot put down C.B. 5.10.

" And what then?"

" My mother was still sitting where she had been when we set out. I went up and spoke to her, and then went on to my tent."

" Can you remember exactly what passed between you?"

" I just said it was very hot and that I was going to lie down. My mother said she would remain where she was. That was all."

" Did anything in her appearance strike you as out of the ordinary?"

" No. At least that is——"

She paused doubtfully, staring at Poirot.

" It is not from me that you can get the answer, mademoiselle," said Poirot quietly.

" I was just considering. I hardly noticed at the time, but now, looking back——"

" Yes?"

Carol said slowly: " It is true—she was a funny colour—her face was very red—more so than usual."

" She might, perhaps, have had a shock of some kind?" Poirot suggested.

" A shock?" she stared at him.

" Yes, she might have had, let us say, some trouble with one of the Arab servants."

" Oh!" Her face cleared. " Yes—she might."

" She did not mention such a thing having happened?"

" N-o—no, nothing at all."

Poirot went on: " And what did you do next, mademoiselle?"

" I went to my tent and lay down for about half an hour. Then I went down to the marquee. My brother and his wife were there reading."

" And what did you do?"

"Oh! I had some sewing to do. And then I picked up a magazine."

"Did you speak to your mother again on your way to the marquee?"

"No. I went straight down. I don't think I even glanced in her direction."

"And then?"

"I remained in the marquee until—until Miss King told us she was dead."

"And that is all you know, mademoiselle?"

"Yes."

Poirot leaned forward. His tone was the same, light and conversational.

"And what did you *feel*, mademoiselle?"

"What did I feel?"

"Yes—when you found that your mother—pardon— your stepmother, was she not?—what did you feel when you found her dead?"

She stared at him.

"I don't understand what you mean!"

"I think you understand very well."

Her eyes dropped. She said uncertainly:

"It was—a great shock."

"Was it?"

The blood rushed to her face. She stared at him helplessly. Now he saw fear in her eyes.

"*Was* it such a great shock, mademoiselle? *Remembering a certain conversation you had with your brother Raymond one night in Jerusalem?*"

His shot proved right. He saw it in the way the colour drained out of her cheeks again.

"You know about that?" she whispered.

"Yes, I know."

"But how—how?"

"Part of your conversation was overheard."

"Oh!" Carol Boynton buried her face in her hands. Her sobs shook the table.

Hercule Poirot waited a minute, then he said quietly:

"You were planning together to bring about your stepmother's death."

Carol sobbed out brokenly: "We were mad—mad—that evening!"

"Perhaps."

" It's impossible for you to understand the state we were in!" She sat up, pushing back the hair from her face. " It would sound fantastic. It wasn't so bad in America—but travelling brought it home to us so."

" Brought what home to you?" His voice was kind now, sympathetic.

" Our being different from—other people! We—we got desperate about it. And there was Jinny."

" Jinny?"

" My sister. You haven't seen her. She was going—well, queer. And mother was making her worse. She didn't seem to realise. We were afraid, Ray and I, that Jinny was going quite, quite mad! And we saw Nadine thought so, too, and that made us more afraid because Nadine knows about nursing and things like that."

" Yes, yes?"

" That evening in Jerusalem things kind of boiled up! Ray was beside himself. He and I got all strung up and it seemed —oh, indeed, it did seem *right* to plan as we did! Mother— mother *wasn't* sane. I don't know what you think, but it *can* seem quite *right*—almost noble—to kill someone!"

Poirot nodded his head slowly. " Yes, it has seemed so, I know, to many. That is proved by history."

" That's how Ray and I felt—that night . . ." She beat her hand on the table. " But we didn't really do it. Of course we didn't do it! When daylight came the whole thing seemed absurd, melodramatic—oh, yes, and wicked too! Indeed, indeed, M. Poirot, mother died perfectly naturally of heart failure. Ray and I had nothing to do with it."

Poirot said quietly: " Will you swear to me, mademoiselle, as you hope for salvation after death, that Mrs. Boynton did not die as the result of any action of yours?"

She lifted her head. Her voice came steady and deep:

" I swear," said Carol, " as I hope for salvation, that I never harmed her. . . ."

Poirot leaned back in his chair.

" So," he said, " that is that."

There was silence. Poirot thoughtfully caressed his superb moustache. Then he said: " What exactly was your plan?"

" Plan?"

" Yes, you and your brother must have had a plan."

In his mind he ticked off the seconds before her answer came. One, two, three.

110

"We had no plan," said Carol at last. "We never got as far as that."

Hercule Poirot got up.

"That is all, mademoiselle. Will you be so good as to send your brother to me?"

Carol rose. She stood undecidedly for a minute.

"M. Poirot, you do—you do believe me?"

"Have I said," asked Poirot, "that I do not?"

"No, but——" She stopped.

He said: "You will ask your brother to come here?"

"Yes."

She went slowly towards the door. She stopped as she got to it, turning round passionately.

"I *have* told you the truth—I have!"

Hercule Poirot did not answer.

Carol Boynton went slowly out of the room.

Chapter 9

POIROT NOTED the likeness between brother and sister as Raymond Boynton came into the room.

His face was stern and set. He did not seem nervous or afraid. He dropped into a chair, stared hard at Poirot, and said: "Well?"

Poirot said gently: "Your sister has spoken with you?"

Raymond nodded. "Yes, when she told me to come here. Of course I realise that your suspicions are quite justified. If our conversation was overheard that night, the fact that my stepmother died rather suddenly certainly *would* seem suspicious! I can only assure you that that conversation was—the madness of an evening! We were, at the time, under an intolerable strain. This fantastic plan of killing my stepmother did—oh, how shall I put it?—it let off steam somehow!"

Hercule Poirot bent his head slowly.

"That," he said, "is possible."

"In the morning, of course, it all seemed—rather absurd! I swear to you, M. Poirot, that I never thought of the matter again!"

Poirot did not answer.

Raymond said quickly:

" Oh, yes, I know that that is easy enough to *say*. I cannot expect you to believe me on my bare word. But consider the facts. I spoke to my mother just a little before six o'clock. She was certainly alive and well then. I went to my tent, had a wash and joined the others in the marquee. From that time onwards neither Carol nor I moved from the place. We were in full sight of everyone. You must see, M. Poirot, that my mother's death was natural—a case of heart failure—it couldn't be anything else! There were servants about, a lot of coming and going. Any other idea is absurd."

Poirot said quietly: " Do you know, Mr. Boynton, that Miss King is of the opinion that when she examined the body—at six-thirty—death had occurred at least an hour and a half and probably *two hours* earlier?"

Raymond stared at him. He looked dumbfounded.

" Sarah said that?" he gasped.

Poirot nodded. " What have you to say now?"

" But—it's impossible!"

" That is Miss King's testimony. Now *you* come and tell me that your mother was alive and well only forty minutes before Miss King examined the body."

Raymond said: " But she was!"

" Be careful, Mr. Boynton."

" Sarah *must* be mistaken! There must be some factor she didn't take into account. Refraction off the rock—something. I can assure you, M. Poirot, that my mother *was* alive at just before six and that I spoke to her."

Poirot's face showed nothing.

Raymond leant forward earnestly.

" M. Poirot, I know how it must seem to you, but look at the thing fairly. You are a biased person. You are bound to be by the nature of things. You live in an atmosphere of crime. Every sudden death must seem to you a possible crime! Can't you realise that your sense of proportion is not to be relied upon? People die every day—especially people with weak hearts—and there is nothing in the least sinister about such deaths."

Poirot sighed. " So you would teach me my business, is that it?"

" No, of course not. But I do think that you are prejudiced —because of that unfortunate conversation. There is nothing really about my mother's death to awaken suspicion except

112

that unlucky hysterical conversation between Carol and myself."

Poirot shook his head. " You are in error," he said. " There is something else. There is the poison taken from Dr. Gerard's medicine chest."

" Poison?" Ray stared at him. *" Poison?"* He pushed his chair back a little. He looked completely stupefied. " Is *that* what you suspect?"

Poirot gave him a minute or two. Then he said quietly, almost indifferently: " Your plan was different—eh?"

" Oh, yes." Raymond answered mechanically. " That's why—this changes everything. . . . I—I can't think clearly."

" What was *your* plan?"

" Our plan? It was——"

Raymond stopped abruptly. His eyes became alert, suddenly watchful.

" I don't think," he said, " that I'll say any more."

" As you please," said Poirot.

He watched the young man out of the room.

He drew his pad towards him and in small, neat characters made a final entry. R.B. 5.55?

Then, taking a large sheet of paper, he proceeded to write. His task completed, he sat back with his head on one side contemplating the result. It ran as follows:

Boyntons and Jefferson Cope leave the camp	3.5 (approx.)
Dr. Gerard and Sarah King leave the camp	3.15 (approx.)
Lady Westholme and Miss Pierce leave the camp	4.15
Nadine Boynton leaves her mother-in-law	
Dr. Gerard returns to camp	4.20 (approx.)
Lennox Boynton returns to camp... ...	4.35
Nadine Boynton returns to camp and talks to Mrs. Boynton	4.40
and goes to marquee	4.50 (approx.)
Carol Boynton returns to camp	5.10
Lady Westholme, Miss Pierce and Mr. Jefferson Cope return to camp ...	5.40
Raymond Boynton returns to camp ...	5.50
Sarah King returns to camp	6.0
Body discovered	6.30

Chapter 10

"I WONDER," said Hercule Poirot. He folded up the list, went to the door and ordered Mahmoud to be brought to him. The stout dragoman was voluble. Words dripped from him in a rising flood.

"Always, always, I am blamed. When anything happens, say always, my fault. Always my fault. When Lady Ellen Hunt sprain her ankle coming down from Place of Sacrifice it my fault, though she would go high-heeled shoes and she sixty at least—perhaps seventy. My life all one misery! Ah! what with miseries and iniquities, Jews do to us——"

At last Poirot succeeded in stemming the flood and in getting in his question.

"Half-past five o'clock, you say? No, I not think any of servants were about then. You see, lunch is late—two o'clock. And then to clear it away. After the lunch all afternoon sleep. Yes, Americans, they not take tea. We all settle sleep by half-past three. At five I who am soul of efficiency—always—always I watch for the comfort of ladies and gentlemen I serving, I come out knowing that time all English ladies want tea. But no one there. They all gone walking. For me, that is very well—better than usual. I can go back sleep. At quarter to six trouble begin—large English lady—very grand lady—come back and want tea although boys are now laying dinner. She makes quite fuss—says water must be boiling—I am to see myself. Ah, my good gentlemen! What a life— what a life! I do all I can—always I blamed—I——"

Poirot asked about the recriminations.

"There is another small matter. The dead lady was angry with one of the boys. Do you know which one it was and what it was about?"

Mahmoud's hands rose to heaven.

"Should I know? But naturally not. Old lady did not complain to me."

"Could you find out?"

"No, my good gentlemen, that would be impossible. None of the boys admit it for a moment. Old lady angry, you say? Then naturally boys would not tell. Abdul say it Mohammed, and Mohammed say it Aziz and Aziz say it Aissa, and so on. They are all very stupid Bedouin—understand nothing."

He took a breath and continued: " Now I, I have advantage of Mission education. I recite to you Keats—Shelley—' Iadadoveandasweedovedied——' "

Poirot flinched. Though English was not his native tongue, he knew it well enough to suffer from the strange enunciation of Mahmoud.

" Superb!" he said hastily. " Superb! Definitely I recommend you to all my friends."

He contrived to escape from the dragoman's eloquence. Then he took his list to Colonel Carbury, whom he found in his office.

Carbury pushed his tie a little more askew and asked: " Got anything?"

Poirot said: " Shall I tell you a theory of mine?"

" If you like," said Colonel Carbury, and sighed. One way and another he heard a good many theories in the course of his existence.

" My theory is that criminology is the easiest science in the world! One has only to let the criminal talk—sooner or later he will tell you everything."

" I remember you said something of the kind before. Who's been telling you things?"

" Everybody." Briefly, Poirot retailed the interviews he had had that morning.

" H'm," said Carbury. " Yes, you've got hold of a pointer or two, perhaps. Pity of it is they all seem to point in opposite directions. Have we got a case, that's what I want to know?"

" No."

Carbury sighed again. " I was afraid not."

" But before nightfall," said Poirot, " you shall have the truth!"

" Well, that's all you ever promised me," said Colonel Carbury. " And I rather doubted you getting that! Sure of it?"

" I am very sure."

" Must be nice to feel like that," commented the other.

If there was a faint twinkle in his eye, Poirot appeared unaware of it. He produced his list.

" Neat," said Colonel Carbury approvingly.

He bent over it.

After a minute or two he said: " Know what I think?"

" I should be delighted if you would tell me."

"Young Raymond Boynton's out of it."

"Ah! you think so?"

"Yes. Clear as a bell what *he* thought. We might have known he'd be out of it. Being, as in detective stories, the most likely person. Since you practically overheard him saying he was going to bump off the old lady—we might have known that meant he was innocent!"

"You read the detective stories, yes?"

"Thousands of them," said Colonel Carbury. He added, and his tone was that of a wistful schoolboy: "I suppose you couldn't do the things the detective does in books? Write a list of significant facts—things that don't seem to mean anything but are really frightfully important—that sort of thing."

"Ah," said Poirot kindly. "You like that kind of detective story? But certainly, I will do it for you with pleasure."

He drew a sheet of paper towards him and wrote quickly and neatly:

SIGNIFICANT POINTS

1. Mrs. Boynton was taking a mixture containing digitalis.
2. Dr. Gerard missed a hypodermic syringe.
3. Mrs. Boynton took definite pleasure in keeping her family from enjoying themselves with other people.
4. Mrs. Boynton, on the afternoon in question, encouraged her family to go away and leave her.
5. Mrs. Boynton was a mental sadist.
6. The distance from the marquee to the place where Mrs. Boynton was sitting is (roughly) two hundred yards.
7. Mr. Lennox Boynton said at first he did not know what time he returned to the camp, but later he admitted having set his mother's wrist-watch to the right time.
8. Dr. Gerard and Miss Ginevra Boynton occupied tents next door to each other.
9. At half-past six, when dinner was ready, a servant was despatched to announce the fact to Mrs. Boynton.

The Colonel perused this with great satisfaction.

"Capital!" he said. "Just the thing! You've made it difficult—and seemingly irrelevant—absolutely the authentic touch! By the way, it seems to me there are one or two rather noticeable omissions. But that, I suppose, is what you tempt the mug with?"

116

Poirot's eyes twinkled a little, but he did not answer.

"Point two, for instance," said Colonel Carbury tentatively. "*Dr. Gerard missed a hypodermic syringe*—yes. He also missed a concentrated solution of digitalis—or something of that kind."

"The latter point," said Poirot, "is not important in the way the absence of his hypodermic syringe is important."

"Splendid!" said Colonel Carbury, his face irradiated with smiles. "I don't get it at all. *I* should have said the digitalis was much more important than the syringe! And what about that servant motif that keeps cropping up—a servant being sent to tell her dinner was ready—and that story of her shaking her stick at a servant earlier in the afternoon? You're not going to tell me one of my poor desert mutts bumped her off after all? Because," added Colonel Carbury sternly, "if so, that would be *cheating*."

Poirot smiled, but did not answer.

As he left the office he murmured to himself:

"Incredible! The English never grow up!"

Chapter 11

SARAH KING sat on a hill-top absently plucking up wild flowers. Dr. Gerard sat on a rough wall of stones near her.

She said suddenly and fiercely: "Why did you start all this? If it hadn't been for *you*——"

Dr. Gerard said slowly: "You think I should have kept silence?"

"Yes."

"Knowing what I knew?"

"You didn't *know*," said Sarah.

The Frenchman sighed. "I did know. But I admit one can never be absolutely sure."

"Yes, one can," said Sarah uncompromisingly.

The Frenchman shrugged his shoulders. "You, perhaps!"

Sarah said: "You had fever—a high temperature—you couldn't be clear-headed about the business. The syringe was probably there all the time. And you may have made a mistake about the digitoxin or one of the servants may have meddled with the case."

Gerard said cynically: "You need not worry! The evidence

is almost bound to be inconclusive. You will see, your friends the Boyntons will get away with it!"

Sarah said fiercely: "I don't want that, either."

He shook his head. "You are illogical!"

"Wasn't it you—" Sarah demanded, "in Jerusalem—who said a great deal about not interfering? And now look!"

"I have not interfered. I have only told what I know!"

"And I say you don't *know* it. Oh dear, there we are, back again! I'm arguing in a circle."

Gerard said gently: "I am sorry, Miss King."

Sarah said in a low voice:

"You see, after all, *they haven't escaped*—any of them! *She's* still there! Even from her grave she can still reach out and hold them. There was something—terrible about her—she's just as terrible now she's dead! I feel—I feel she's *enjoying* all this!"

She clenched her hands. Then she said in an entirely different tone, a light everyday voice: "That little man's coming up the hill."

Dr. Gerard looked over his shoulder.

"Ah! he comes in search of us, I think."

"Is he as much of a fool as he looks?" asked Sarah.

Dr. Gerard said gravely: "He is not a fool at all."

"I was afraid of that," said Sarah King.

With sombre eyes she watched the uphill progress of Hercule Poirot.

He reached them at last, uttered a loud 'ouf' and wiped his forehead. Then he looked sadly down at his patent leather shoes.

"Alas!" he said. "This stony country! My poor shoes."

"You can borrow Lady Westholme's shoe-cleaning apparatus," said Sarah unkindly. "And her duster. She travels with a kind of patent housemaid's equipment."

"That will not remove the scratches, mademoiselle." Poirot shook his head sadly.

"Perhaps not. Why on earth do you wear shoes like that in this sort of country?"

Poirot put his head a little on one side.

"I like to have the appearance *soigné*," he said.

"I should give up trying for that in the desert," said Sarah.

"Women do not look their best in the desert," said Dr. Gerard dreamily. "Miss King here, yes—she always looks neat and well-turned out. But that Lady Westholme in her

118

great thick coats and skirts and those terribly unbecoming riding breeches and boots—*quelle horreur de femme!* And the poor Miss Pierce—her clothes so limp, like faded cabbage leaves, and the chains and the beads that clink! Even young Mrs. Boynton, who is a good-looking woman, is not what you call *chic*! Her clothes are uninteresting."

Sarah said restively: "Well, I don't suppose M. Poirot climbed up here to talk about clothes!"

"True," said Poirot. "I came to consult Dr. Gerard—his opinion should be of value to me—and yours, too, mademoiselle—you are young and up to date in your psychology. I want to know, you see, all that you can tell me of Mrs. Boynton."

"Don't you know all that by heart now?" asked Sarah.

"No. I have a feeling—more than a feeling—a certainty that the mental equipment of Mrs. Boynton is very important in this case. Such types as hers are no doubt familiar to Dr. Gerard."

"From my point of view she was certainly an interesting study," said the doctor.

"Tell me."

Dr. Gerard was nothing loth. He described his own interest in the family group, his conversation with Jefferson Cope, and the latter's complete misreading of the situation.

"He is a sentimentalist, then," said Poirot.

"Oh, essentially! He has ideals—based, really, on a deep instinct of laziness. To take human nature at its best, and the world as a pleasant place is undoubtedly the easiest course in life! Jefferson Cope has, consequently, not the least idea what people are really like."

"That might be dangerous sometimes," said Poirot.

Dr. Gerard went on: "He persisted in regarding what I may describe as 'the Boynton situation' as a case of mistaken devotion. Of the underlying hate, rebellion, slavery and misery he had only the faintest notion."

"It is stupid, that," Poirot commented.

"All the same," went on Dr. Gerard, "even the most wilfully obtuse of sentimental optimists cannot be quite blind. I think, on the journey to Petra, Mr. Jefferson Cope's eyes were being opened."

And he described the conversation he had had with the American on the morning of Mrs. Boynton's death.

"That is an interesting story, that story of a servant girl,"

119

said Poirot thoughtfully. " It throws light on the old woman's methods."

Gerard said: " It was altogether an odd strange morning, that! You have not been to Petra, M. Poirot. If you go you must certainly climb to the Place of Sacrifice. It has an—how shall I say?—an atmosphere!" He described the scene in detail, adding: " Mademoiselle here sat like a young judge, speaking of the sacrifice of one to save many. You remember, Miss King?"

Sarah shivered. " Don't! Don't let's talk of that day."

" No, no," said Poirot. " Let us talk of events further back in the past. I am interested, Dr. Gerard, in your sketch of Mrs. Boynton's mentality. What I do not quite understand is this, having brought her family into absolute subjection, why did she then arrange this trip abroad where surely there was danger of outside contacts and of her authority being weakened?"

Dr. Gerard leaned forward excitedly.

" But, *mon vieux,* that is just it! Old ladies are the same all the world over. They get bored! If their speciality is playing patience, they sicken of the patience they know too well. They want to learn a new patience. And it is just the same with an old lady whose recreation (incredible as it may sound) is the dominating and tormenting of human creatures! Mrs. Boynton—to speak of her as *une dompteuse*—had tamed her tigers. There was perhaps some excitement as they passed through the stage of adolescence. Lennox's marriage to Nadine was an adventure. But then, suddenly, all was stale. Lennox is so sunk in melancholy that it is practically impossible to wound or distress him. Raymond and Carol show no signs of rebellion. Ginevra—ah! *la pauvre Ginevra* —she, from her mother's point of view, gives the poorest sport of all. For Ginevra has found a way of escape! She escapes from reality into fantasy. The more her mother goads her, the more easily she gets a secret thrill out of being a persecuted heroine! From Mrs. Boynton's point of view it is all deadly dull. She seeks, like Alexander, new worlds to conquer. And so she plans the voyage abroad. There will be the danger of her tamed beasts rebelling, there will be opportunities for inflicting fresh pain! It sounds absurd, does it not, but it was so! She wanted a new thrill."

Poirot took a deep breath. " It is perfect, that. Yes, I see exactly what you mean. *It was so*. It all fits in. She

120

chose to live dangerously, *la maman* Boynton—and she paid the penalty!"

Sarah leaned forward, her pale, intelligent face very serious. "You mean," she said, "that she drove her victims too far and—and they turned on her—or—or one of them did?"

Poirot bowed his head.

Sarah said, and her voice was a little breathless:

"*Which of them?*"

Poirot looked at her, at her hands clenched fiercely on the wild flowers, at the pale rigidity of her face.

He did not answer—was indeed saved from answering, for at that moment Gerard touched his shoulder and said: "Look."

A girl was wandering along the side of the hill. She moved with a strange rhythmic grace that somehow gave the impression that she was not quite real. The gold red of her hair shone in the sunlight, a strange secretive smile lifted the beautiful corners of her mouth. Poirot drew in his breath.

He said: "How beautiful. . . . How strangely movingly beautiful. . . . That is how Ophelia should be played—like a young goddess straying from another world, happy because she has escaped out of the bondage of human joys and griefs."

"Yes, yes, you are right," said Gerard. "It is a face to dream of, is it not? *I* dreamt of it. In my fever I opened my eyes and saw that face—with its sweet, unearthly smile. . . . It was a good dream. I was sorry to wake. . . ."

Then, with a return to his commonplace manner:

"That is Ginevra Boynton," he said.

Chapter 12

In another minute the girl had reached them.

Dr. Gerard performed the introduction.

"Miss Boynton, this is M. Hercule Poirot."

"Oh." She looked at him uncertainly. Her fingers joined together, twined themselves uneasily in and out. The enchanted nymph had come back from the country of enchantment. She was now just an ordinary awkward girl, slightly nervous and ill at ease.

121

Poirot said: "It is a piece of good fortune meeting you here, mademoiselle. I tried to see you in the hotel."

"Did you?"

Her smile was vacant. Her fingers began plucking at the belt of her dress. He said gently:

"Will you walk with me a little way?"

She moved docilely enough, obedient to his whim.

Presently she said, rather unexpectedly, in a queer, hurried voice:

"You are—you are a detective, aren't you?"

"Yes, mademoiselle."

"A very well-known detective?"

"The best detective in the world," said Poirot, stating it as a simple truth, no more, no less.

Ginevra Boynton breathed very softly:

"You have come here to protect me?"

Poirot stroked his moustache thoughtfully. He said:

"Are you, then, in danger, mademoiselle?"

"Yes, yes." She looked round with a quick, suspicious glance. "I told Dr. Gerard about it in Jerusalem. He was very clever. He gave no sign at the time. But he followed me —to that terrible place with the red rocks." She shivered. "They meant to kill me there. I have to be continually on my guard."

Poirot nodded gently and indulgently.

Ginevra Boynton said: "He is kind—and good. He is in love with me!"

"Yes?"

"Oh, yes. He says my name in his sleep. . . ." Her voice softened—again a kind of trembling, unearthly beauty hovered there. "I saw him—lying there turning and tossing—and saying my name. . . . I stole away quietly." She paused. "I thought, perhaps, *he* had sent for you? I have a terrible lot of enemies, you know. They are all round me. Sometimes they are *disguised*."

"Yes, yes," said Poirot gently. "But you are safe here— with all your family round you."

She drew herself up proudly.

"They are *not* my family! I have nothing to do with them. I cannot tell you who I really am—that is a great secret. It would surprise you if you knew."

He said gently: "Was your mother's death a great shock to you, mademoiselle?"

Ginevra stamped her feet.

"I tell you—she *wasn't* my mother! My enemies paid her to pretend she was and to see I did not escape!"

"Where were you on the afternoon of her death?"

"I was in the tent. . . . It was hot in there, but I didn't dare come out. . . . *They* might have got me. . . ." She gave a little quiver. "One of them—looked into my tent. He was disguised, but I knew him. I pretended to be asleep. The Shiekh had sent him. The Shiekh wanted to kidnap me, of course."

For a few moments Poirot walked in silence, then he said: "They are very pretty, these histories you recount to yourself?"

She stopped. She glared at him. "They're *true*. They're all *true*." Again she stamped an angry foot.

"Yes," said Poirot, "they are certainly ingenious."

She cried out: "They are true—*true*——"

Then, angrily, she turned from him and ran down the hillside. Poirot stood looking after her. In a minute or two he heard a voice close behind him.

"What did you say to her?"

Poirot turned to where Dr. Gerard, a little out of breath, stood beside him. Sarah was coming towards them both, but she came at a more leisurely pace.

Poirot answered Gerard's question.

"I told her," he said, "that she had imagined to herself some pretty stories."

The doctor nodded his head thoughtfully.

"And she was angry? That is a good sign. It shows, you see, that she has not yet completely passed through the door. She still knows that it is *not* the truth! I shall cure her."

"Ah, you are undertaking a cure?"

"Yes. I have discussed the matter with young Mrs. Boynton and her husband. Ginevra will come to Paris and enter one of my clinics. Afterwards she will have her training for the stage."

"The stage?"

"Yes—there is a possibility there for her of great success. And that is what she needs—what she *must* have! In many essentials she has the same nature as her mother."

"No!" cried Sarah, revolted.

"It seems impossible to you, but certain fundamental traits are the same. They were both born with a great yearning for importance; they both demand that their personality shall impress! This poor child has been thwarted and suppressed at every turn; she has been given no outlet for her fierce ambition, for her love of life, for the expression of her vivid romantic personality." He gave a little laugh. "*Nous allons changer tout ça!*"

Then, with a little bow, he murmured: "You will excuse me?" And he hurried down the hill after the girl.

Sarah said: "Dr. Gerard is tremendously keen on his job."

"I perceive his keenness," said Poirot.

Sarah said, with a frown: "All the same, I can't bear his comparing her to that horrible old woman—although, once— I felt sorry for Mrs. Boynton myself."

"When was that, mademoiselle?"

"That time I told you about in Jerusalem. I suddenly felt as though I'd got the whole business wrong. You know that feeling one has sometimes when just for a short time you see everything the other way round? I got all het-up about it and went and made a fool of myself!"

"Oh, no—not that!"

Sarah, as always when she remembered her conversation with Mrs. Boynton, was blushing acutely.

"I felt all exalted as though I had a mission! And then later, when Lady W. fixed a fishy eye on me and said she had seen me talking to Mrs. Boynton, I thought she had probably overheard, and I felt the *most* complete ass."

Poirot said: "What exactly was it that old Mrs. Boynton said to you? Can you remember the exact words?"

"I think so. They made rather an impression on me. '*I never forget,*' that's what she said. '*Remember that. I've never forgotten anything—not an action, not a name, not a face.*'" Sarah shivered. "She said it so *malevolently*—not even looking at me. I feel—I feel as if, even now, I can hear her. . . ."

Poirot said gently: "It impressed you very much?"

"Yes. I'm not easily frightened—but sometimes I dream of her saying just those words and her evil, leering, triumphant face. Ugh!" She gave a quick shiver. Then she turned suddenly to him.

"M. Poirot, perhaps I ought not to ask, but have you come to a conclusion about this business? Have you found out anything definite?"

"Yes."

He saw her lips tremble as she asked. "What?"

"I have found out to whom Raymond Boynton spoke that night in Jerusalem. It was to his sister Carol."

"Carol—of course!"

Then she went on: "Did you tell him—did you ask him——"

It was no use. She could not go on. Poirot looked at her gravely and compassionately. He said quietly:

"It means—so much to you, mademoiselle?"

"It means just everything!" said Sarah. Then she squared her shoulders. "But I've got to *know*."

Poirot said quietly: "He told me that it was a hysterical outburst—no more! That he and his sister were worked up. He told me that in daylight such an idea appeared fantastic to them both."

"I see. . . ."

Poirot said gently: "Miss Sarah, will you not tell me what it is you fear?"

Sarah turned a white despairing face upon him.

"That afternoon—we were together. And he left me saying—saying he wanted to do something *now*—while he had the courage. I thought he meant just to—to tell her. But supposing he meant. . . ."

Her voice died away. She stood rigid, fighting for control.

Chapter 13

NADINE BOYNTON came out of the hotel. As she hesitated uncertainly, a waiting figure sprang forward.

Mr. Jefferson Cope was immediately at his lady's side.

"Shall we walk up this way? I think it's the pleasantest." She acquiesced.

They walked along and Mr. Cope talked. His words came freely if a trifle monotonously. It is not certain whether he perceived that Nadine was not listening. As they turned aside on to the stony flower-covered hill-side, she interrupted him.

"Jefferson, I'm sorry. I've got to talk to you."

Her face had grown pale.

"Why, certainly, my dear. Anything you like, but don't distress yourself."

She said: "You're cleverer than I thought. You know, don't you, what I'm going to say?"

"It is undoubtedly true," said Mr. Cope, "that circumstances alter cases. I do feel, very profoundly, that in the present circumstances decisions may have to be reconsidered." He sighed. "You've got to go right ahead, Nadine, and do just what you feel."

She said with real emotion: "You're so *good*, Jefferson. So patient! I feel I've treated you very badly. I really have been downright mean to you."

"Now, look here, Nadine, let's get this right. I've always known what my limitations were where you were concerned. I'd had the deepest affection and respect for you ever since I've known you. All I want is your happiness. That's all I've ever wanted. Seeing you unhappy has very nearly driven me crazy. And I may say that I've blamed Lennox. I've felt that he didn't deserve to keep you if he didn't value your happiness a little more than he seemed to do."

Mr. Cope took a breath and went on:

"Now I'll admit that after travelling with you to Petra, I felt that perhaps Lennox wasn't quite so much to blame as I thought. He wasn't so much selfish where you were concerned, as too unselfish where his mother was concerned. I don't want to say anything against the dead, but I do think that your mother-in-law was perhaps an unusually difficult woman."

"Yes, I think you may say that," murmured Nadine.

"Anyway," went on Mr. Cope, "you came to me yesterday and told me that you'd definitely decided to leave Lennox. I applaud your decision. It wasn't right—the life you were leading. You were quite honest with me. You didn't pretend to be more than just mildly fond of me. Well, that was all right with me. All I asked was the chance to look after you and treat you as you should be treated. I may say that afternoon was one of the happiest afternoons in my life."

Nadine cried out: "I'm sorry—I'm sorry."

"No, my dear, because all along I had a kind of feeling that it wasn't real. I felt it was quite on the cards that you would have changed your mind by the next morning. Well, things are different now. You and Lennox can lead a life of your own."

Nadine said quietly: "Yes. I can't leave Lennox. Please forgive me."

"Nothing to forgive," declared Mr. Cope. "You and I will go back to being old friends. We'll just forget about that afternoon."

Nadine placed a gentle hand on his arm. "Dear Jefferson, thank you. I'm going to find Lennox now."

She turned and left him. Mr. Cope went on alone.

Nadine found Lennox sitting at the top of the Græco-Roman theatre. He was in such a brown study that he hardly noticed her till she sank breathless at his side. "Lennox."

"Nadine." He half turned.

She said: "We haven't been able to talk until now. But you know, don't you, that I am not leaving you?"

He said gravely: "Did you ever really mean to, Nadine?"

She nodded. "Yes. You see, it seemed to be the only possible thing left to do. I hoped—I hoped that you would come after me. Poor Jefferson, how mean I have been to him."

Lennox gave a sudden curt laugh.

"No, you haven't. Anyone who is as unselfish as Cope ought to be given full scope for his nobility! And you were right, you know, Nadine. When you told me that you were going away with him you gave me the shock of my life! You know, honestly, I think I must have been going queer or something lately. Why the hell didn't I snap my fingers in mother's face and go off with you when you wanted me to?"

She said gently: "You couldn't, my dear, you couldn't."

Lennox said musingly: "Mother was a damned queer character. . . . I believe she'd got us all half hypnotised."

"She had."

Lennox mused a minute or two longer. Then he said: "When you told me that afternoon—it was just like being hit a crack on the head! I walked back half dazed, and then, suddenly I saw what a damned fool I'd been! I realised that there was only one thing to be done if I didn't want to lose you."

He felt her stiffen. His tone became grimmer.

"I went and——"

"Don't. . . ."

He gave her a quick glance.

"I went and—argued with her." He spoke with a complete change of tone—careful and rather toneless. "I told her that I got to choose between her and you—and that I chose you."

There was a pause.

He repeated, in a tone of curious self-approval:

"Yes, that's what I said to her."

Chapter 14

POIROT MET two people on his way home. The first was Mr. Jefferson Cope.

" M. Hercule Poirot? My name's Jefferson Cope."

The two men shook hands ceremoniously.

Then, falling into step beside Poirot, Mr. Cope explained: " It's just got round to me that you're making a kind of routine inquiry into the death of my old friend Mrs. Boynton. That certainly was a shocking business. Of course, mind you, the old lady ought never to have undertaken such a fatiguing journey. But she was headstrong, M. Poirot. Her family could do nothing with her. She was by way of being a household tyrant—had had her own way too long, I guess. It certainly is true that what she said went. Yes, sir, that certainly was true."

There was a momentary pause.

" I'd just like to tell you, M. Poirot, that I'm an old friend of the Boynton family. Naturally they're all a good deal upset over this business; they're a trifle nervous and highly strung, too, you know, so if there are any arrangements to be made— necessary formalities, arrangements for the funeral—transport of the body to Jerusalem, why, I'll take as much trouble as I can off their hands. Just call upon me for anything that needs doing."

" I am sure the family will appreciate your offer," said Poirot. He added, " You are, I think, a special friend of young Mrs. Boynton's."

Mr. Jefferson Cope went a little pink.

" Well, we won't say much about that, M. Poirot. I hear you had an interview with Mrs. Lennox Boynton this morning, and she may have given you a hint how things were between us, but that's all over now. Mrs. Boynton is a very fine woman and she feels that her first duty is to her husband in his sad bereavement."

There was a pause. Poirot received the information by a delicate gesture of the head. Then he murmured:

" It is the desire of Colonel Carbury to have a clear statement concerning the afternoon of Mrs. Boynton's death. Can you give me an account of that afternoon?"

" Why, certainly. After our luncheon and a brief rest we set out for a kind of informal tour round. We escaped. I'm glad to say, without that pestilential dragoman. That man's just crazy on the subject of the Jews. I don't think he's quite sane on that point. Anyway, as I was saying, we set out. It was then that I had my interview with Nadine. Afterwards she wished to be alone with her husband to discuss matters with him. I went off on my own, working gradually back towards the camp. About half-way there I met the two English ladies who had been on the morning expedition—one of them's an English peeress, I understand?"

Poirot said that such was the case.

" Ah, she's a fine woman, a very powerful intellect and very well informed. The other seemed to me rather a weak sister—and she looked about dead with fatigue. That expedition in the morning was very strenuous for an elderly lady, especially when she doesn't like heights. Well, as I was saying, I met these two ladies and was able to give them some information on the subject of the Nabateans. We went around a bit and got back to the camp about six. Lady Westholme insisted on having tea and I had the pleasure of having a cup with her—the tea was kind of weak, but it had an interesting flavour. Then the boys laid the table for supper and sent out to the old lady only to find that she was sitting there dead in her chair."

" Did you notice her as you walked home?"

" I did notice she was there—it was her usual seat in the afternoon and evening, but I didn't pay special attention. I was just explaining to Lady Westholme the conditions of our slump. I had to keep an eye on Miss Pierce, too. She was so tired she kept turning her ankles."

" Thank you, Mr. Cope. May I be so indiscreet as to ask if Mrs. Boynton is likely to have left a large fortune?"

" A very considerable one. That is to say, strictly speaking, it was not hers to leave. She had a life interest in it and at her death it is divided between the late Elmer Boynton's children. Yes, they will all be very comfortably off now."

" Money," murmured Poirot, " makes a lot of difference. How many crimes have been committed for it?"

Mr. Cope looked a little startled.

" Why, that's so, I suppose," he admitted.

Poirot smiled sweetly and murmured: " But there are so

many motives for murder, are there not? Thank you, Mr. Cope, for your kind co-operation."

"You're welcome, I'm sure," said Mr. Cope. "Do I see Miss King sitting up there? I think I'll go and have a word with her."

Poirot continued to descend the hill.

He met Miss Pierce fluttering up it.

She greeted him breathlessly.

"Oh, M. Poirot, I'm so glad to meet you. I've been talking to that very odd girl—the youngest one, you know. She has been saying the strangest things—about enemies, and some Shiekh that wanted to kidnap her and how she has spies all round her. Really, it sounded *most* romantic! Lady Westholme says it is all nonsense and that she once had a red-headed kitchenmaid who told lies just like that, but I think sometimes that Lady Westholme is rather *hard*. And after all, it might be true, mightn't it, M. Poirot? I read some years ago that one of the Czar's daughters was not killed in the Revolution in Russia, but escaped secretly to America. The Grand Duchess Tatiana, I think it was. If so, this *might* be her daughter, mightn't it? She *did* hint at something royal—and she has a look, don't you think? Rather Slavonic—those cheek-bones. How thrilling it would be!"

Poirot said somewhat sententiously: "It is true that there are many strange things in life."

"I didn't really take in this morning who you were," said Miss Pierce, clasping her hands. "Of course you are that *very* famous detective! I read *all* about the ABC case. It was so *thrilling*. I had actually a post as governess near Doncaster at the time."

Poirot murmured something. Miss Pierce went on with growing agitation.

"That is why I felt that perhaps—I had been wrong—this morning. One must always tell *everything*, must one not? Even the *smallest* detail, however unrelated it may *seem*. Because, of course, if *you* are mixed up in this, poor Mrs. Boynton *must* have been murdered! I see that now! I suppose Mr. Mah Mood—I cannot remember his name—but the dragoman, I mean—I suppose he could not be a *Bolshevik agent*? Or even, perhaps, Miss King? I believe many *quite* well-brought-up girls of *good* family belong to these dreadful Communists! That's why I wondered if I *ought* to tell you—

130

because, you see, it was rather *peculiar* when one comes to think of it."

"Precisely," said Poirot. "And therefore you will tell me all about it."

"Well, it's not really anything very much. It's only that on the next morning after the discovery I was up rather early—and I looked out of my tent to see the effect of the sunrise you know (only, of course, it wasn't actually sunrise because the sun must have risen quite an hour before). But it was *early*——"

"Yes, yes. And you saw?"

"That's the curious thing—at least, at the time it didn't *seem* much. It was only that I saw that Boynton girl come out of her tent and fling something right out into the stream—nothing in *that*, of course, but it *glittered*—in the sunlight! As it went through the air. It *glittered*, you know."

"Which Boynton girl was it?"

"I think it was the one they call Carol—a very nice-looking girl—so like her brother—really they might be *twins*. Or, of course, it *might* have been the youngest one. The sun was in my eyes, so I couldn't quite see. But I don't think the hair was red—just bronze. I'm so fond of that coppery-bronze hair! Red hair always says *carrots* to me!" She tittered.

"And she threw away a brightly glittering object?" said Poirot.

"Yes. And, of course, as I said, I didn't think much of it *at the time*. But later I walked along the stream and Miss King was there. And there amongst a lot of other very unsuitable things—even a tin or two—I saw a little bright metal box—not an exact square—a sort of long square, if you understand what I mean——"

"But yes, I understand perfectly. About so long?"

"Yes, how *clever* of you! And I thought to myself, ' I suppose *that's* what the Boynton girl threw away, but it's a nice little box.' And just out of curiosity I picked it up and opened it. It had a kind of syringe inside—the same thing they stuck into my arm when I was being innoculated for typhoid. And I thought how curious to throw it away like that because it didn't seem broken or anything. But just as I was wondering, Miss King spoke behind me. I hadn't heard her come up. And she said, ' Oh, thank you—that's my hypodermic. I was coming to look for it.' So I gave it to her, and she went back to the camp with it."

Miss Pierce paused and then went on hurriedly:

" And, of course, I expect there is *nothing in it*—only it *did* seem a little curious that Carol Boynton should throw away Miss King's syringe. I mean, it was odd, if you know what I mean. Though, of course, I expect there is a very good explanation."

She paused, looking expectantly at Poirot.

His face was grave. " Thank you, mademoiselle. What you have told me may not be important in itself, but I will tell you this! It completes my case! Everything is now clear and in order."

" Oh, really?" Miss Pierce looked as flushed and pleased as a child.

Poirot escorted her to the hotel.

Back in his own room he added one line to his memorandum. Point No. 10. "*I never forget. Remember that. I've never forgotten anything. . . .*"

"*Mais oui,*" he said. " It is all clear now!"

Chapter 15

" MY PREPARATIONS are complete," said Hercule Poirot.

With a little sigh he stepped back a pace or two and contemplated his arrangement of one of the unoccupied hotel bedrooms.

Colonel Carbury, leaning inelegantly against the bed which had been pushed against the wall, smiled as he puffed at his pipe. " Funny feller, aren't you, Poirot?" he said. " Like to dramatise things."

" Perhaps—that is true," admitted the little detective. " But indeed it is not all self-indulgence. If one plays a comedy, one must first set the scene."

" Is this a comedy?"

" Even if it is a tragedy—there, too, the *décor* must be correct."

Colonel Carbury looked at him curiously.

" Well," he said, " it's up to you! I don't know what you're driving at. I gather, though, that you've *got* something."

" I shall have the honour to present to you what you asked me for—the truth!"

132

" Do you think we can get a conviction?"

" That, my friend, I did not promise you."

" True enough. Maybe I'm glad you haven't. It depends."

" My arguments are mainly psychological," said Poirot.

Colonel Carbury sighed. " I was afraid they might be."

" But they will convince you," Poirot reassured him. " Oh, yes, they will convince you. The truth, I have always thought, is curious and beautiful."

" Sometimes," said Colonel Carbury, " it's damned unpleasant."

" No, no." Poirot was earnest. " You take there the personal view. Take instead the abstract, the detached point of vision. Then the absolute logic of events is fascinating and orderly."

" I'll try to look on it that way," said the Colonel.

Poirot glanced at his watch, a large grotesque turnip of a watch.

" But yes, indeed, it belonged to my grandfather."

" Thought it might have done."

" It is time to commence our proceedings," said Poirot. " You, *mon Colonel*, will sit here behind this table in an official position."

" Oh, all right," Carbury grunted. " You don't want me to put my uniform on, do you?"

" No, no. If you would permit that I straightened your tie." He suited the action to the word. Colonel Carbury grinned again, sat down in the chair indicated and a moment later, unconsciously, tweaked his tie round under his left ear again.

" Here," continued Poirot, slightly altering the position of the chairs, " we place *la famille Boynton*.

" And over here," he went on, " we will place the three outsiders who have a definite stake in the case. Dr. Gerard, on whose evidence the case for the prosecution depends. Miss Sarah King, who has two separate interests in the case, a personal one, and that of medical examiner. Also Mr. Jefferson Cope, who was on intimate terms with the Boyntons and so may be definitely described as an interested party."

He broke off. " Aha—here they come."

He opened the door to admit the party.

Lennox Boynton and his wife came in first. Raymond and Carol followed. Ginevra walked by herself, a faint, faraway smile on her lips. Dr. Gerard and Sarah King brought up the rear. Mr. Jefferson Cope was a few minutes late and came in with an apology.

When he had taken his place Poirot stepped forward.

"Ladies and gentlemen," he said, "this is an entirely informal gathering. It has come about through the accident of my presence in Amman. Colonel Carbury did me the honour to consult me——"

Poirot was interrupted. The interruption came from what was seemingly the most unlikely quarter. Lennox Boynton said suddenly and pugnaciously:

"Why? Why the devil should he bring you into this business?"

Poirot waved a hand gracefully.

"Me, I am often called in in cases of sudden death."

Lennox Boynton said: "Doctors send for you whenever there is a case of heart failure?"

Poirot said gently: "Heart failure is such a very loose and unscientific term."

Colonel Carbury cleared his throat. It was an official noise. He spoke in an official tone.

"Best to make it quite clear. Circumstance of death reported to me. Very natural occurrence. Weather unusually hot—journey a very trying one for an elderly lady in bad health. So far all quite clear. But Dr. Gerard came to me and volunteered a statement——"

He looked inquiringly at Poirot. Poirot nodded.

"Dr. Gerard is a very eminent physician with a world-wide reputation. Any statement he makes is bound to be received with attention. Dr. Gerard's statement was as follows. On the morning after Mrs Boynton's death he noticed that a certain quantity of a powerful drug acting on the heart was missing from his medical supplies. On the previous afternoon he had noted the disappearance of a hypodermic syringe. Syringe was returned during the night. Final point—there was a puncture on the dead woman's wrist corresponding to the mark of a hypodermic syringe."

Colonel Carbury paused.

"In these circumstances I considered that it was the duty of those in authority to inquire into the matter. M. Hercule Poirot was my guest and very considerately offered his highly specialised services. I gave him full authority to make any investigations he pleased. We are assembled here now to hear his report on the matter."

134

There was silence—a silence so acute that you could have heard—as the saying is—a pin drop. Actually somebody did drop what was probably a shoe in the next room. It sounded like a bomb in the hushed atmosphere.

Poirot cast a quick glance at the little group of three people on his right, then turned his gaze to the five people huddled together on his left—a group of people with frightened eyes.

Poirot said quietly: " When Colonel Carbury mentioned this business to me, I gave him my opinion as an expert. I told him that it might not be possible to bring proof—such proof as would be admissible in a court of law—but I told him very definitely that I was sure I could arrive at the truth—simply by questioning the people concerned. For let me tell you this, my friends, to investigate a crime it is only necessary to let the guilty party or parties *talk*—always, in the end, they tell you what you want to know!" He paused.

" So, in this case, although you have lied to me, you have also, unwittingly, told me the truth."

He heard a faint sigh, the scrape of a chair on the floor to his right, but he did not look round. He continued to look at the Boyntons'

" First, I examined the possibility of Mrs. Boynton having died a natural death—and I decided against it. The missing drug—the hypodermic syringe—and above all, the attitude of the dead lady's family all convinced me that that supposition could not be entertained.

" Not only was Mrs. Boynton killed in cold blood—but every member of her family was aware of the fact! Collectively they reacted as guilty parties.

" But there are degrees in guilt. I examined the evidence carefully with a view to ascertaining whether the murder—yes, it was *murder*!—had been committed by the old lady's family *acting on a concerted plan*.

" There was, I may say, overwhelming motive. One and all stood to gain by her death—both in the financial sense—for they would at once attain financial independence and indeed enjoy very considerable wealth—and also in the sense of being freed from what had become an almost insupportable tyranny.

" To continue: I decided, almost immediately, that the concerted theory would not hold water. The stories of the Boynton family did not dovetail neatly into each other, and no system of workable alibis had been arranged. The facts seemed more to suggest that one—or possibly two—members of the family had acted in collusion and that the others were accessories after the fact. I next considered which particular member or members—were indicated. Here, I may say, I was inclined to be biased by a certain piece of evidence known only to myself."

Here Poirot recounted his experience in Jerusalem.

"Naturally, that pointed very strongly to Mr. Raymond Boynton as the prime mover in the affair. Studying the family, I came to the conclusion that the most likely recipient of his confidences that night would be his sister Carol. They strongly resembled each other in appearance and temperament, and so would have a keen bond of sympathy and they also possessed the nervous rebellious temperament necessary for the conception of such an act. That their motive was partly unselfish—to free the whole family and particularly their younger sister—only made the planning of the deed more plausible." Poirot paused a minute.

Raymond Boynton half opened his lips, then shut them again. His eyes looked steadily at Poirot with a kind of dumb agony in them.

"Before I go into the case against Raymond Boynton, I would like to read to you a list of significant points which I drew up and submitted to Colonel Carbury this afternoon.

SIGNIFICANT POINTS

1. Mrs. Boynton was taking a mixture containing digitalin.
2. Dr. Gerard missed a hypodermic syringe.
3. Mrs. Boynton took definite pleasure in keeping her family from enjoying themselves with other people.
4. Mrs. Boynton, on the afternoon in question, encouraged her family to go away and leave her.
5. Mrs. Boynton is a mental sadist.
6. The distance from the marquee to the place where Mrs. Boynton was sitting is (roughly) two hundred yards.
7. Mr. Lennox Boynton said at first he did not know what time he returned to the camp, but later he admitted having set his mother's wrist-watch to the right time.
8. Dr. Gerard and Miss Ginevra Boynton occupied tents next door to each other.
9. At half-past six, when dinner was ready, a servant was despatched to announce the fact to Mrs. Boynton.

136

10. Mrs. Boynton, in Jerusalem, used these words: 'I never forget. Remember that. I've never forgotten anything.'

"Although I have numbered the points separately, occasionally they can be bracketed in pairs. That is the case, for instance, with the first two. *Mrs. Boynton taking a mixture containing digitalin. Dr. Gerard had missed a hypodermic syringe.* Those two points were the first thing that struck me about the case, and I may say to you that I found them most extraordinary—and quite irreconcilable. You do not see what I mean? No matter. I will return to the point presently. Let it suffice that I noted those two points as something that had definitely got to be explained satisfactorily.

" I will conclude now with my study of the possibility of Raymond Boynton's guilt. The following are the facts. He had been heard to discuss the possibility of taking Mrs. Boynton's life. He was in a condition of great nervous excitement. He had—mademoiselle will forgive me "—he bowed apologetically to Sarah—" just passed through a moment of great emotional crisis. That is, he had fallen in love. The exaltation of his feelings might lead him to act in one of several ways. He might feel mellowed and softened towards the world in general, including his stepmother—he might feel the courage at last to defy her and shake off her influence—or he might find just the additional spur to turn his crime from theory to practice. That is the psychology! Let us now examine the *facts*.

" Raymond Boynton left the camp with the others about three-fifteen. Mrs. Boynton was then alive and well. Before long Raymond and Sarah King had a *tête-à-tête* interview. Then he left her. According to him, he returned to the camp at ten minutes to six. He went up to his mother, exchanged a few words with her, then went to his tent and afterwards down to the marquee. He says that at ten minutes to six, *Mrs. Boynton was alive and well.*

" But we now come to a fact which directly contradicts that statement. At half-past six Mrs. Boynton's death was discovered by a servant. Miss King, who holds a medical degree, examined her body and she swears definitely that at that time, though she did not pay any special attention to the time when death had occurred, it had *most certainly and decisively* taken

137

place at least an hour (and probably *a good deal more*) before six o'clock.

" We have here, you see, two conflicting statements. Setting aside the possibility that Miss King may have made a mistake——"

Sarah interrupted him. " I don't make mistakes. That is, if I had, I would admit to it."

Her tone was hard and clear.

Poirot bowed to her politely.

" Then there are only two possibilities—either Miss King or Mr. Boynton are lying! Let us examine Raymond Boynton's reasons for so doing. Let us assume that Miss King was *not* mistaken and *not* deliberately lying. What, then, was the sequence of events? Raymond Boynton returns to the camp, sees his mother sitting at the mouth of her cave, goes up to her and finds she is dead. What does he do? Does he call for help? Does he immediately inform the camp of what has happened? No, he waits a minute or two, then passes on to his tent and joins his family in the marquee and *says nothing*. Such conduct is exceedingly curious, is it not?"

Raymond said in a nervous, sharp voice:

" It would be idiotic, of course. That ought to show you that my mother was alive and well as I've said. Miss King was flustered and upset and made a mistake."

" One asks oneself," said Poirot, calmly sweeping on, " whether there could possibly be a reason for such conduct? It seems, on the face of it, that Raymond Boynton *cannot be guilty*, since at the only time he was known to approach his stepmother that afternoon *she had already been dead for some time*. Now, supposing, therefore, that Raymond Boynton is *innocent*, can we explain his conduct?

" And I say, that on the assumption that he is innocent, we can! For I remember that fragment of conversation I overheard. '*You do see, don't you, that she's got to be killed?*' He comes back from his walk and finds her dead and at once his guilty memory envisages a certain possibility. The plan has been carried out—not by him—but by his fellow-planner. *Tout simplement*—he suspects that his sister, Carol Boynton, is guilty."

" It's a lie," said Raymond in a low, trembling voice.

Poirot went on: " Let us now take the possibility of Carol Boynton being the murderess. What is the evidence against

138

her? She has the same highly-strung temperament—the kind of temperament that might see such a deed coloured with heroism. It was she to whom Raymond Boynton was talking that night in Jerusalem. Carol Boynton returned to the camp at ten minutes past five. According to her own story she went up and spoke to her mother. No one saw her do so. The camp was deserted—the boys were asleep. Lady Westholme, Miss Pierce and Mr. Cope were exploring caves out of sight of the camp. There was no witness of Carol Boynton's possible action. The time would agree well enough. The case, then, against Carol Boynton is a perfectly possible one." He paused. Carol had raised her head. Her eyes looked steadily and sorrowfully into his.

"There is one other point. The following morning, very early, Carol Boynton was seen to throw something into the stream. There is reason to believe that that something was a hypodermic syringe."

"Comment?" Dr. Gerard looked up surprised. "But my hypodermic was *returned*. Yes, yes, I have it now."

Poirot nodded vigorously.

"Yes, yes. This second hypodermic, it is very curious—very interesting. I have been given to understand that this hypodermic belonged to Miss King. Is that so?"

Sarah paused for a fraction of a second.

Carol spoke quickly: "It was not Miss King's syringe," she said. "It was mine."

"Then you admit throwing it away, mademoiselle?"

She hesitated just a second.

"Yes, of course. Why shouldn't I?"

"Carol!" It was Nadine. She leaned forward, her eyes wide and distressed. "Carol. . . . Oh, I don't understand. . . ."

Carol turned and looked at her. There was something hostile in her glance.

"There's nothing *to* understand! I threw away an old hypodermic. I never touched the—the poison."

Sarah's voice broke in: "It is quite true what Miss Pierce told you, M. Poirot. It *was* my syringe."

Poirot smiled.

"It is very confusing, this affair of the hypodermic—and yet, I think, it could be explained. Ah, well, we have now two cases made out—the case for the innocence of Raymond

Boynton—the case for the guilt of his sister Carol. But me, I am scrupulously fair. I look always on both sides. Let us examine what occurred if Carol Boynton was innocent.

"She returns to the camp, she goes up to her stepmother, and she finds her—shall we say—dead! What is the first thing she will think? She will suspect that her brother Raymond may have killed her. She does not know what to do. So she says nothing. And presently, about an hour later, Raymond Boynton returns and having presumably spoken to his mother, *says nothing of anything being amiss.* Do you not think that then her suspicions would become certainties? Perhaps she goes to his tent and finds there a hypodermic syringe. Then, indeed, she is *sure*! She takes it quickly and hides it. Early in the morning she flings it as far away as she can.

"There is one more indication that Carol Boynton is innocent. She assures me when I question her that she and her brother never seriously intended to carry out their plan. I ask her to swear—and she swears immediately and with the utmost solemnity that she is not guilty of the crime! You see, that is the way she puts it. She does not swear that *they* are not guilty. She swears for *herself*, not her brother—and thinks that I will not pay special attention to the pronoun.

"*Eh bien*, that is the case for the innocence of Carol Boynton. And now let us go back a step and consider not the innocence but the possible guilt of Raymond. Let us suppose that Carol is speaking the truth, that Mrs. Boynton was alive at five-ten. Under what circumstances can Raymond be guilty? We can suppose that he killed his mother at ten minutes to six when he went up to speak to her. There were boys about the camp, true, but the light was fading. It might have been managed, but it then follows that Miss King lied. Remember, she came back to the camp only five minutes after Raymond. From the distance she would see him go up to his mother. Then, when later she is found dead, Miss King realises that *Raymond has killed her*, and to save him, she lies —knowing that Dr. Gerard is down with fever and cannot expose her lie!"

"I did *not* lie!" said Sarah clearly.

"There is yet another possibility. Miss King, as I have said, reached the camp a few minutes after Raymond. If Raymond Boynton found his mother alive, it may have been *Miss King* who administered the fatal injection. She believed that Mrs. Boynton was fundamentally evil. She may have seen herself as a just executioner. That would equally well explain her lying about the time of death."

Sarah had grown very pale. She spoke in a low, steady voice.

"It is true that I spoke of the expediency of one person dying to save many. It was the Place of Sacrifice that suggested the idea to me. But I can swear to you that I never harmed that disgusting old woman —no would the idea of doing so ever have entered my head!"

"And yet," said Poirot softly. "one of you two *must be lying*."

Raymond Boynton shifted in his chair. He cried out impetuously:

"You win, M. Poirot! I'm the liar. Mother was dead when I went up to her. It—it quite knocked me out. I'd been going, you see, to have it out with her. To tell her that from henceforth I was a free agent. I was—all set, you understand. And there she was—dead! Her hand all cold and flabby. And I thought—just what you said. I thought maybe Carol— you see, there was the mark on her wrist——"

Poirot said quickly: "That is the one point on which I am not completely informed. What was the method you counted on employing? You *had* a method—and it was connected with a hypodermic syringe. That much I know. If you want me to believe you, you must tell me the rest."

Raymond said hurriedly: "It was a way I read in a book— an English detective story—you stuck an empty hypodermic syringe into someone and it did the trick. It sounded perfecly scientific. I—I thought we'd do it that way."

"Ah," said Poirot. "I comprehend. And you purchased a syringe?"

"No. As a matter of fact I pinched Nadine's."

Poirot shot a quick look at her. "The syringe that is in your baggage in Jerusalem?" he murmured.

A faint colour showed in the young woman's face.

"I—I wasn't sure what had become of it," she murmured.

Poirot murmured: "You are so quick-witted, madame."

Chapter 16

THERE WAS a pause. Then clearing his throat with a slightly affected sound, Poirot went on:

"We have now solved the mystery of what I might term *the second hypodermic*. That belonged to Mrs. Lennox Boynton, was taken by Raymond Boynton before leaving Jerusalem, was taken from Raymond by Carol after the discovery of Mrs. Boynton's dead body, was thrown away by her, found by Miss Pierce, and claimed by Miss King as hers. I presume Miss King has it now."

"I have," said Sarah.

"So that when you said it was yours just now, you were doing what you told us you do not do—you told a lie."

Sarah said calmly: "That's a different kind of lie. It isn't—it isn't a *professional* lie."

Gerard nodded appreciation.

"Yes, it is a point that. I understand you perfectly, mademoiselle."

"Thanks," said Sarah.

Again Poirot cleared his throat.

"Let us now review our time-table. Thus:"

Boyntons and Jefferson Cope leave the camp	3.5	(approx.)
Dr. Gerard and Sarah King leave the camp	3.15	(approx.)
Lady Westholme and Miss Pierce leave the camp	4.15	
Dr. Gerard returns to camp	4.20	(approx.)
Lennox Boynton returns to camp... ...	4.35	
Nadine Boynton returns to camp and talks to Mrs. Boynton	4.40	
Nadine Boynton leaves her mother-in-law and goes to marquee	4.50	(approx.)
Carol Boynton returns to camp	5.10	
Lady Westholme, Miss Pierce and Mr. Jefferson Cope return to camp ...	5.40	
Raymond Boynton returns to camp ...	5.50	
Sarah King returns to camp	6.0	
Body discovered	6.30	

" There is, you will notice, a gap of twenty minutes between four-fifty when Nadine Boynton left her mother-in-law and five-ten when Carol returned. Therefore, if Carol is speaking the truth, Mrs. Boynton must have been killed in that twenty minutes.

" Now who could have killed her? At that time Miss King and Raymond Boynton were together. Mr. Cope (not that he had any perceivable motive for killing her) has an alibi. He was with Lady Westholme and Miss Pierce. Lennox Boynton was with his wife in the marquee. Dr. Gerard was groaning with fever in his tent. The camp is deserted, the boys are asleep. It is a suitable moment for a crime! Was there a person who could have committed it?"

His eyes went thoughtfully to Ginevra Boynton.

" *There was one person.* Ginevra Boynton was in her tent all the afternoon. That is what we have been told—but actually there is evidence that she was *not* in her tent all the time. Ginevra Boynton made a very significant remark. She said that Dr. Gerard spoke her name in his fever. And Dr. Gerard has also told us that he dreamt in his fever of Ginevra Boynton's face. But it was not a dream! It was actually her face he saw, standing there by his bed. He thought it an effect of fever—but it was the truth. Ginevra was in Dr. Gerard's tent. Is it not possible that she had come to put back the hypodermic syringe after using it?"

Ginevra Boynton raised her head with its crown of red-gold hair. Her wide beautiful eyes stared at Poirot. They were singularly expressionless. She looked like a vague saint.

" *Ah, ça non!*" cried Dr. Gerard.

" Is it, then, so psychologically impossible?" inquired Poirot.

The Frenchman's eyes dropped.

Nadine Boynton said sharply: " It's quite impossible!"

Poirot's eyes came quickly round to her.

" Impossible, madame?"

" Yes." She paused, bit her lip, then went on, " I will not hear of such a disgraceful accusation against my young sister-in-law. We—all of us—know it to be impossible."

Ginevra moved a little on her chair. The lines of her mouth relaxed into a smile—the touching, innocent half-unconscious smile of a very young girl.

Nadine said again: " Impossible."

143

Her gentle face had hardened into lines of determination. The eyes that met Poirot's were hard and unflinching.

Poirot leaned forward in what was half a bow.

"Madame is very intelligent," he said.

Nadine said quietly: "What do you mean by that, M. Poirot?"

"I mean, madame, that all along I have realised that you have what I believe is called an 'excellent headpiece'."

"You flatter me."

"I think not. All along you have envisaged the situation calmly and collectively. You have remained on outwardly good terms with your husband's mother, deeming that the best thing to be done, but inwardly you have judged and condemned her. I think that some time ago you realised that the only chance for your husband's happiness was for him to make an effort to leave home—strike out on his own no matter how difficult and penurious such a life might be. You were willing to take all risks and you endeavoured to influence him to exactly that course of action. But you failed, madame. Lennox Boynton had no longer *the will to freedom*. He was content to sink into a condition of apathy and melancholy.

"Now I have no doubt at all, madame, but that you love your husband. Your decision to leave him was not actuated by a greater love for another man. It was, I think, a desperate venture undertaken as a last hope. A woman in your position could only try three things. She could try appeal. That, as I have said, failed. She could threaten to leave herself. But it is possible that even that threat would not have moved Lennox Boynton. It would plunge him deeper in misery, but it would not cause him to rebel. There was one last desperate throw. *You could go away with another man.* Jealousy and the instinct of possession is one of the most deeply rooted fundamental instincts in man. You showed your wisdom in trying to reach that deep underground savage instinct. If Lennox Boynton would let you go without an effort to another man— then he must indeed be beyond human aid, and you might as well then try to make a new life for yourself elsewhere.

"But let us suppose that even that last desperate remedy failed. Your husband was terribly upset at your decision, but in spite of that he did not, as you had hoped, react as a primitive man might have done with an uprush of the possessive instinct. Was there anything at all that could save your husband from his own rapidly failing mental condition? Only

144

one thing. *If his stepmother were to die,* it might not be too late. He might be able to start life anew as a free man, building up in himself independence and manliness once more."

Poirot paused, then repeated gently: "If your mother-in-law were to die. . . ."

Nadine's eyes were still fixed on him. In an unmoved gentle voice she said: "You are suggesting that I helped to bring that event about, are you not? But you cannot do so, M. Poirot. After I had broken the news of my impending departure to Mrs. Boynton, I went straight to the marquee and joined Lennox. I did not leave it again until my mother-in-law was found dead. Guilty of her death I may be, in the sense that I gave her a shock—that, of course, presupposes a natural death. But if, as you say (though so far you have no direct evidence of it and cannot have until an autopsy has taken place) she was deliberately killed, then *I* had no opportunity of doing so."

Poirot said: "You did not leave the marquee again until your mother-in-law was found dead. That is what you have just said. That, Mrs. Boynton, was one of the points I found curious about this case."

"What do you mean?"

"It is here on my list. Point nine. At half-past six, when dinner was ready, a servant was despatched to announce the fact to Mrs. Boynton."

Raymond said: "I don't understand."

Carol said: "No more do I."

Poirot looked from one to the other of them.

"You do not, eh? 'A servant was sent'—why a *servant?* Were you not, all of you, most assiduous in your attendance on the old lady as a general rule? Did not one or other of you always escort her to meals? She was infirm. It was difficult for her to rise from a chair without assistance. Always one or other of you was at her elbow. I suggest then, that on dinner being announced the natural thing would have been for one or other of her family to go out and help her. But not one of you offered to do so. You all sat there, paralysed, watching each other, wondering, perhaps, why no one went."

Nadine said sharply: "All this is absurd, M. Poirot! We were all tired that evening. We ought to have gone, I admit, but—on that evening—we just didn't!"

"Precisely—precisely—*on that particular evening!* You,"
145

madame, did perhaps more waiting on her than anyone else. It was one of the duties that you accepted mechanically. But that evening you did not offer to go out to help her in. Why? That is what I asked myself—why? And I tell you my answer. *Because you knew quite well that she was dead.* . . .

"No, no, do not interrupt me, madame." He raised an impassioned hand. "You will now listen to me—Hercule Poirot! There were witnesses to your conversation with your mother-in-law. Witnesses who could *see* but could not *hear*! Lady Westholme and Miss Pierce were a long way away. They saw you *apparently* having a conversation with your mother-in-law, but what actual evidence is there of what occurred? I will propound to you instead a little theory. You have brains, madame. If in your quiet unhurried fashion you have decided on—shall we say the *elimination* of your husband's mother—you will carry it out with intelligence and with due preparation. You have access to Dr. Gerard's tent during his absence on the morning excursion. You are fairly sure that you will find a suitable drug. Your nursing training helps you there. You choose digitoxin—the same kind of drug that the old lady is taking—you also take his hypodermic syringe since, to your annoyance, your own has disappeared. You hope to replace the syringe before the doctor notices its absence."

"Before proceeding to carry out your plan, you make one last attempt to stir your husband into action. You tell him of your intention to marry Jefferson Cope. Though your husband is terribly upset he does not react as you had hoped —so you are forced to put your plan of murder into action. You return to the camp exchanging a pleasant natural word with Lady Westholme and Miss Pierce as you pass. You go up to where your mother-in-law is sitting. You have the syringe with the drug in it ready. It is easy to seize her wrist and—proficient as you are with your nurse's training—force home the plunger. It is done before your mother-in-law realises what you are doing. From far down the valley the others only see you talking to her, bending over her. Then deliberately you go and fetch a chair and sit there apparently engaged in an amicable conversation for some minutes. Death must have been almost instantaneous. It is a dead woman to whom you sit talking, but who shall guess that? Then you put away the chair and go down to the marquee, where you find your husband reading a book. And you are

146

careful not to leave that marquee! Mrs. Boynton's death, you
are sure, will be put down to heart trouble. (It will, indeed, be
due to heart trouble.) In only one thing have your plans
gone astray. You cannot return the syringe to Dr. Gerard's
tent because the doctor is in there shivering with malaria—
and although you do not know it, he has *already missed the
syringe*. That, madame, was the flaw in an otherwise perfect
crime."

There was silence—a moment's dead silence—then Lennox
Boynton sprang to his feet.

"No," he shouted. "That's a damned lie. Nadine did
nothing. She couldn't have done anything. My mother—my
mother was already dead."

"Ah?" Poirot's eyes came gently round to him. "So,
after all, it was *you* who killed her, Mr. Boynton."

Again a moment's pause—then Lennox dropped back into
his chair and raised trembling hands to his face.

"Yes—that's right—I killed her."

"You took the digitoxin from Dr. Gerard's tent?"

"Yes."

"When?"

"As—as—you said—in the morning."

"And the syringe?"

"The syringe? Yes."

"Why did you kill her?"

"Can you ask?"

"I *am* asking, Mr. Boynton!"

"But you *know*—my wife was leaving me—with Cope——"

"Yes, but you only learnt that in the *afternoon*."

Lennox stared at him. "Of course. When we were
out——"

"But you took the poison and the syringe in the *morning*
—*before* you knew?"

"Why the hell do you badger me with questions?" He
paused and passed a shaking hand across his forehead.
"What does it matter, anyway?"

"It matters a great deal. I advise you, Mr. Lennox
Boynton, to tell me the truth."

"The truth?" Lennox stared at him.

"That is what I said—the truth."

"By God, I will," said Lennox suddenly. "But I don't
know whether you will believe me." He drew a deep breath.
"That afternoon, when I left Nadine, I was absolutely all to
147

pieces. I'd never dreamed she'd go from me to someone else. I was—I was nearly mad! I felt as though I was drunk or recovering from a bad illness."

Poirot nodded. He said: "I noted Lady Westholme's description of your gait when you passed her. That is why I knew your wife was not speaking the truth when she said she told you *after* you were both back at the camp. Continue, Mr. Boynton."

"I hardly knew what I was doing. . . . But as I got near, my brain seemed to clear. It flashed over me that I had only myself to blame! I'd been a miserable worm! I ought to have defied my stepmother and cleared out years ago. And it came to me that it mightn't be too late even now. There she was, the old devil, sitting up like an obscene idol against the red cliffs. I went right up to have it out with her. I meant to tell her just what I thought and to announce that I was clearing out. I had a wild idea I might get away at once that evening—clear out with Nadine and get as far as Ma'an, anyway, that night."

"Oh, Lennox—my dear——"

It was a long, soft sigh.

He went on: "And then, my God—you could have struck me down with a touch! She was dead. Sitting there—dead. . . . I—I didn't know what to do—I was dumb—dazed—everything I was going to shout out at her bottled up inside me—turning to lead—I can't explain. . . . Stone—that's what it felt like—being turned to stone. I did something mechanically—I picked up her wristwatch—it was lying in her lap—and put it round her wrist—her horrid limp dead wrist. . . ."

He shuddered. "God—it was awful. . . . Then I stumbled down, went into the marquee. I ought to have called someone, I suppose—but I couldn't. I just sat there, turning the pages—waiting. . . ."

He stopped.

"You won't believe that—you can't. Why didn't I call someone? Tell Nadine? I don't know."

Dr. Gerard cleared his throat.

"Your statement is perfectly plausible, Mr. Boynton," he said. "You were in a bad nervous condition. Two severe shocks administered in rapid succession would be quite enough to put you in the condition you have described. It is the Weissenhalter reaction—best exemplified in the case of a bird that has dashed its head against a window. Even after its

148

recovery it refrains instinctively from all action—giving itself time to readjust the nerve centres—I do not express myself well in English, but what I mean is this: *You could not have acted any other way.* Any decisive action of any kind would have been quite impossible for you! You passed through a period of mental paralysis."

He turned to Poirot.

" I assure you, my friend, that is so!"

" Oh, I do not doubt it," said Poirot. " There was a little fact I had already noted—the fact that Mr. Boynton had replaced his mother's wrist-watch—that was capable of two explanations—it might have been a cover for the actual deed, or it might have been observed and misinterpreted by Mrs. Boynton. She returned only five minutes after her husband. She must therefore have seen that action. When she got up to her mother-in-law and found her dead with a mark of a hypodermic syringe on her wrist she would naturally jump to the conclusion that her husband had committed the deed— that her announcement of her decision to leave him had produced a reaction in him different from that for which she had hoped. Briefly, Nadine Boynton believed that she had inspired her husband to commit murder."

He looked at Nadine. " That is so, madame?"

She bowed her head. Then she asked:

" Did you *really* suspect me, M. Poirot?"

" I thought you were a possibility, madame."

She leaned forward.

" And now? *What really happened, M. Poirot?"*

Chapter 17

" WHAT REALLY happened?" Poirot repeated.

He reached behind him, drew forward a chair and sat down. His manner was now friendly—informal.

" It is a question, is it not? For the digitoxin *was* taken— the syringe *was* missing—there *was* the mark of a hypodermic on Mrs. Boynton's wrist.

" It is true that in a few days' time we shall know definitely —the autopsy will tell us—whether Mrs. Boynton died of an overdose of digitalis or not. But then it may be too late! It would be better to reach the truth to-night—while the murderer is here under our hand."

Nadine raised her head sharply.

"You mean that you still believe—that one of us—here in this room. . . ." Her voice died away.

Poirot was slowly nodding to himself.

"The truth, that is what I promised Colonel Carbury. And so, having cleared our path we are back again where I was earlier in the day, writing down a list of printed facts and being faced straightway with two glaring inconsistencies."

Colonel Carbury spoke for the first time. "Suppose, now, we hear what they are?" he suggested.

Poirot said with dignity: "I am about to tell you. We will take once more those first two facts on my list. *Mrs. Boynton was taking a mixture of digitalis and Dr. Gerard missed a hypodermic syringe.* Take those facts and set them against the undeniable fact (with which I was immediately confronted) that the Boynton family showed unmistakably guilty reactions. It would seem, therefore, certain that one of the Boynton family *must* have committed the crime! And yet, those two facts I mentioned were al. *against* that theory. For, you see, to take a concentrated solution of digitalis—that, yes, it is a clever idea, because Mrs. Boynton was already taking the drug. But what would a member of her family do then? *Ah, ma foi!* there was only one sensible thing to do. Put the poison *into her bottle of medicine*! That is what anyone, anyone with a grain of sense *and who had access to the medicine* would certainly do!

"Sooner or later Mrs. Boynton takes a dose and dies—and even if the digitalin is discovered in the bottle it may be set down as a mistake of the chemist who made it up. Certainly nothing can be proved!

"Why, then, *the theft of the hypodermic needle*?

"There can be only two explanations of that—either Dr. Gerard overlooked the syringe and it was never stolen, or else the syringe was taken because the murderer had *not* got access to the medicine—that is to say the murderer was *not* a member of the Boynton family. Those two first facts point overwhelmingly to an *outsider* as having committed the crime!

"I saw that—but I was puzzled, as I say, by the strong evidences of guilt displayed by the Boynton family. Was it possible that, *in spite of that consciousness of guilt*, the Boynton family were *innocent*? I set out to prove—not the guilt —but the *innocence* of those people!

" That is where we stand now. The murder was committed by an outsider—that is, *by someone who was not sufficiently intimate with Mrs. Boynton to enter her tent or to handle her medicine bottle.*"

He paused.

" There are three people in this room who are, technically, outsiders, but who have a definite connection with the case.

" Mr. Cope, whom we will consider first, has been closely associated with the Boynton family for some time. Can we discover motive and opportunity on his part? It seems not. Mrs. Boynton's death has affected him adversely—since it has brought about the frustration of certain hopes. Unless Mr. Cope's motive was an almost fanatical desire to benefit others, we can find no reason for his desiring Mrs. Boynton's death. (Unless, of course, there is a motive about which we are entirely in the dark. We do not know what Mr. Cope's dealings with the Boynton family have been.)"

Mr. Cope said with dignity: " This seems to me a little far-fetched, M. Poirot. You must remember I had absolutely no opportunity for committing this deed and, in any case I hold very strong views as to the sanctity of human life."

" Your position certainly seems impeccable," said Poirot with gravity. " In a work of fiction you would be strongly suspected on that account."

He turned a little in his chair. " We now come to Miss King. Miss King had a certain amount of motive and she had the necessary medical knowledge and is a person of character and determination, but since she left the camp before three-thirty with the others and did not return to it until six o'clock, it seems difficult to see where she could have got her opportunity.

" Next we must consider Dr. Gerard. Now here we must take into account the actual time that the murder was committed. According to Mr. Lennox Boynton's last statement, his mother was dead at four thirty-five. According to Lady Westholme and Miss Pierce, she was alive at four-sixteen when they started on their walk. That leaves *exactly twenty minutes* unaccounted for. Now, as these two ladies walked *away* from the camp, Dr. Gerard passed them going to it. There is no one to say *what Dr. Gerard's movements were when he reached the camp* because the two ladies' backs were towards it. They were walking *away* from it. *Therefore it is perfectly possible for Dr. Gerard to have committed the crime.* Being a doctor, he could easily counterfeit the appearance of malaria. There is, I should say, a possible motive. Dr. Gerard might have wished to save a certain person whose reason (perhaps more vital a loss than loss of life) was in danger, and he may have considered the sacrifice of an old and worn-out life worth it!"

" Your ideas," said Dr. Gerard, " are fantastic!"

Without taking any notice, Poirot went on:

" But if so, *why did Gerard call attention to the possibility of foul play?* It is quite certain that, but for his statement to Colonel Carbury, Mrs. Boynton's death would have been put down to natural causes. It was *Dr. Gerard* who first pointed out the possibility of murder. That, my friends," said Poirot, " does not make common sense!"

" Doesn't seem to," said Colonel Garbury gruffly.

" There is one more possibility," said Poirot. " Mrs. Lennox Boynton just now negatived strongly the possibility of her young sister-in-law being guilty. The force of her objection lay in the fact that she knew her mother-in-law to be dead at the time. But remember this, Ginevra Boynton was at the camp all the afternoon. And there was a moment—a moment when Lady Westholme and Miss Pierce were walking away from the camp and before Dr. Gerard had returned to it . . ."

Ginevra stirred. She leaned forward, staring into Poirot's face with a strange, innocent, puzzled stare.

" *I* did it? You think I did it?"

Then suddenly, with a movement of swift incomparable beauty, she was up from her chair and had flung herself across the room and down on her knees beside Dr. Gerard, clinging to him, gazing up passionately into his face.

" No, no, don't let them say it! They're making the walls close round me again! It's not true! I never did anything! They are my enemies—they want to put me in prison—to shut me up. You *must* help me. *You* must help me!"

" There, there, my child." Gently the doctor patted her head. Then he addressed Poirot.

" What you say is nonsense—absurd."

" Delusions of persecution?" murmured Poirot.

" Yes ; but she could never have done it that way. She would have done it, you must perceive, *dramatically*—a dagger —something flamboyant—spectacular—never this cool, calm

152

logic! I tell you, my friends, it is *so*. This was a reasoned crime—a sane crime."

Poirot smiled. Unexpectedly he bowed. *"Je suis entièrement de votre avis,"* he said smoothly.

Chapter 18

"COME," said Hercule Poirot. "We have still a little way to go! Dr. Gerard has invoked the psychology. So let us now examine the psychological side of the case. We have taken the *facts*, we have established a *chronological sequence of events*, we have heard the *evidence*. There remains—the psychology. And the most important psychological evidence concerns the dead woman—it is the psychology of Mrs. Boynton herself that is the most important thing in this case.

"Take from my list of specified facts points three and four. *Mrs. Boynton took definite pleasure in keeping her family from enjoying themselves with other people. Mrs. Boynton, on the afternoon in question, encouraged her family to go away and leave her.*

"These two facts, they contradict each other flatly! Why, on this particular afternoon, should Mrs. Boynton suddenly display a complete reversal of her usual policy? Was it that she felt a sudden warmth of the heart—an instinct of benevolence? That, it seems to me from all I have heard, was extremely unlikely! Yet there must have been a *reason*. What was that reason?

"Let us examine closely the character of Mrs. Boynton. There have been many different accounts of her. She was a tyrannical old martinet—she was a mental sadist—she was an incarnation of evil—she was crazy. Which of these views is the true one?

"I think myself that Sarah King came nearest to the truth when in a flash of inspiration in Jerusalem she saw the old lady as intensely pathetic. But not only pathetic—*futile!*

"Let us, if we can, think ourselves into the mental condition of Mrs. Boynton. A human creature born with immense ambition, with a yearning to dominate and to impress her personality on other people. She neither sublimated that intense craving for power—nor did she seek to master it—no, *mesdames and messieurs—she fed it!* But in the end—listen

153

well to this—in the *end* what did it amount to? She was not a great power! She was not feared and hated over a wide area! *She was the petty tyrant of one isolated family!* And as Dr. Gerard said to me—she became bored like any other old lady with her hobby and she sought to extend her activities and to amuse herself by making her dominance more precarious! But that led to an entirely different aspect of the case! By coming abroad, she realised for the first time how extremely insignificant she was!

" And now we come directly to point number ten—the words spoken to Sarah King in Jerusalem. Sarah King, you see, had put her finger on the truth. She had revealed fully and uncompromisingly the pitiful futility of Mrs. Boynton's scheme of existence! And now listen very carefully—all of you—to what her exact words to Miss King were. Miss King has said that Mrs. Boynton spoke ' *so malevolently—not even looking at me.*' And this is what she actually said, ' *I've never forgotten anything—not an action, not a name, not a face.*'

" Those words made a great impression on Miss King. Their extraordinary intensity and the loud hoarse tone in which they were uttered! So strong was the impression that they left on her mind that I think she quite failed to realise their extraordinary significance!

" Do you see that significance, any of you?" He waited a minute. " It seems not. . . . But, *mes amis,* does it escape you that those words *were not a reasonable answer at all* to what Miss King had just been saying? ' *I've never forgotten anything—not an action, not a name, not a face.*' It does not make *sense!* If she had said, ' I never forget impertinence '—something of that kind—but no—*a face* is what she said. . . .

" Ah!" cried Poirot, beating his hands together. " But it leaps to the eye! Those words, *were not meant for Miss King at all!* They were addressed to *someone else* standing *behind* Miss King."

He paused, noting their expressions.

" Yes, it leaps to the eye! That was, I tell you, a psychological moment in Mrs. Boynton's life! She had been *exposed to herself* by an intelligent young woman! She was full of baffled fury—and at that moment she *recognised* someone—a *face* from the past—a victim delivered into her hands!

" We are back, you see, at the *outsider!* And *now* the meaning of Mrs. Boynton's unexpected amiability on the afternoon of her death is clear. *She wanted to get rid of her family because*—to use a vulgarity—*she had other fish to fry!* She wanted the field left clear for an interview with a new victim. . . .

"Now, from that new standpoint, let us consider the events of the afternoon! The Boynton family go off. Mrs. Boynton sits up by her cave. Now let us consider very carefully the evidence of Lady Westholme and Miss Pierce. The latter is an unreliable witness, she is unobservant and very suggestible. Lady Westholme, on the other hand, is perfectly clear as to her facts and meticulously observant. Both ladies agree on *one* fact! *An Arab, one of the servants, approaches Mrs. Boynton, angers her in some way and retires hastily.* Lady Westholme stated definitely that the servant had first been into the tent occupied by Ginevra Boynton, but you may remember that *Dr. Gerard's* tent was next door to Ginevra's. It is possible that it was *Dr. Gerard's* tent the Arab entered. . . ."

Colonel Carbury said: "D'you mean to tell me that one of those Bedouin fellows of mine murdered an old lady by sticking her with a hypodermic? Fantastic!"

"Wait, Colonel Carbury, I have not yet finished. Let us agree that the Arab *might* have come from Dr. Gerard's tent and not Ginevra Boynton's. What is the next thing? Both ladies agree that they could not see his face clearly enough to identify him and that they did not hear what was said. That is understandable. The distance between the marquee and the ledge was about two hundred yards. Lady Westholme gave a clear description of the man otherwise, describing in detail his ragged breeches and the untidiness with which his puttees were rolled."

Poirot leaned forward.

"And that, my friends, *was very odd indeed*! Because if she *could not see his face* or hear what was said, *she could not possibly have noticed the state of his breeches and puttees*! Not at two hundred yards!

"It was an error, that, you see! It suggested a curious idea to me. *Why* insist so on the ragged breeches and untidy puttees? Could it be because the breeches were *not* torn and the *puttees were non-existent*? Lady Westholme and Miss Pierce both saw the man—but from where they were sitting *they could not see each other*. That is shown by the fact that Lady Westholme *came to see* if Miss Pierce was awake and found her sitting in the entrance of her tent."

155

"Good lord," said Colonel Carbury, suddenly sitting up very straight. "Are you suggesting——?"

"I am suggesting that, having ascertained just what Miss Pierce (the only witness likely to be awake) was doing, Lady Westholme returned to her tent, put on her riding breeches, boots and khaki-coloured coat, made herself an Arab head-dress with her checked duster and a skein of knitting wool and that, thus attired, she went boldly up to Dr. Gerard's tent, looked in his medicine chest, selected a suitable drug, took the hypodermic, filled it and went boldly up to her victim.

"Mrs. Boynton may have been dozing. Lady Westholme was quick. She caught her by the wrist and injected the stuff. Mrs. Boynton half cried out—tried to rise—then sank back. The 'Arab' hurried away with every evidence of being ashamed and abashed. Mrs. Boynton shook her stick, tried to rise, then fell back into her chair.

"Five minutes later Lady Westholme rejoins Miss Pierce and comments on the scene she has just witnessed, *impressing her own version of it on the other*. Then they go for a walk, pausing below the ledge where Lady Westholme shouts up to the old lady. She receives no answer. Mrs. Boynton is dead —but she remarks to Miss Pierce, '*Very rude just to snort at us like that!*' Miss Pierce accepts the suggestion—she has often heard Mrs. Boynton receive a remark with a snort— she will swear quite sincerely if necessary that she actually *heard* it. Lady Westholme has sat on committees often enough with women of Miss Pierce's type to know exactly how her own eminence and masterful personality can influence them. The only point where her plan went astray was the replacing of the syringe. Dr. Gerard returning so soon upset her scheme. She hoped he might not have noticed its absence, or might think he had overlooked it, and she put it back during the night."

He stopped.

Sarah said: "But *why*? Why should Lady Westholme want to kill old Mrs. Boynton?"

"Did you not tell me that Lady Westholme had been quite near you in Jerusalem when you spoke to Mrs. Boynton? It was to Lady Westholme that Mrs. Boynton's words were addressed. '*I've never forgotten anything—not an action, not a name, not a face.*' Put that with the fact that Mrs. Boynton *had been a wardress in a prison* and you can get a very

156

shrewd idea of the truth. Lord Westholme met his wife on a voyage back from *America*. Lady Westholme before her marriage had been a criminal and had served a prison sentence.

" You see the terrible dilemma she was in? Her career, her ambitions, her social position—all at stake! What the crime was for which she served a sentence in prison we do not yet know (though we soon shall), but it must have been one that would effectually blast her political career if it was made public. And remember this, *Mrs. Boynton was not an ordinary blackmailer.* She did not want money. She wanted the pleasure of torturing her victim for a while and then she would have enjoyed revealing the truth in the most spectacular fashion! No, while Mrs. Boynton lived, Lady Westholme was not safe. She obeyed Mrs. Boynton's instructions to meet her at Petra (I thought it strange all along that a woman with such a sense of her own importance as Lady Westholme should have preferred to travel as a mere tourist), but in her own mind she was doubtless revolving ways and means of murder. She saw her chance and carried it out boldly. She only made two slips. One was to say a little too much—the description of the torn breeches—which first drew my attention to her, and the other was when she mistook Dr. Gerard's tent and looked first into the one where Ginevra was lying half asleep. Hence the girl's story—half make-believe, half true—of a Sheikh in disguise. She put it the wrong way round, obeying her instinct to distort the truth by making it more dramatic, but the indication was quite significant enough for me."

He paused.

" But we shall soon know. I obtained Lady Westholme's fingerprints to-day without her being aware of the fact. If these are sent to the prison where Mrs. Boynton was once a wardress, we shall soon know the truth when they are compared with the files."

He stopped.

In the momentary stillness a sharp sound was heard.

" What's that?" asked Dr. Gerard.

" Sounded like a shot to me," said Colonel Carbury, rising to his feet quickly. " In the next room. Who's got that room, by the way?"

Poirot murmured: " I have a little idea—it is the room of Lady Westholme. . . ."

Epilogue

EXTRACT from the *Evening Shout*:

We regret to announce the death of Lady Westholme, M.P., the result of a tragic accident. Lady Westholme, who was fond of travelling in out-of-the-way countries, always took a small revolver with her. She was cleaning this when it went off accidentally and killed her. Death was instantaneous. The deepest sympathy will be felt for Lord Westholme, etc., etc.

ON A warm June evening five years later Sarah Boynton and her husband sat in the stalls of a London theatre. The play was *Hamlet*. Sarah gripped Raymond's arm as Ophelia's words came floating over the footlights:

> *How should I your true love know*
> *From another one?*
> *By his cockle hat and staff,*
> *And his sandal shoon.*
>
> *He is dead and gone, lady,*
> *He is dead and gone;*
> *At his head a grass-green turf;*
> *At his heels a stone.*

O, ho!

A lump rose in Sarah's throat. That exquisite witless beauty, that lovely unearthly smile of one gone beyond trouble and grief to a region where only a floating mirage was truth. . . .

Sarah said to herself: " She's lovely. . . ."

That haunting, lilting voice, always beautiful in tone, but now disciplined and modulated to be the perfect instrument.

Sarah said with decision as the curtain fell at the end of the act: " Jinny's a great actress—a great—great actress!"

Later they sat round a supper-table at the Savoy. Ginevra, smiling, remote, turned to the bearded man by her side.

"I was good, wasn't I, Theodore?"

"You were wonderful, *chérie.*"

A happy smile floated on her lips.

She murmured: "*You* always believed in me—you always knew I could do great things—sway multitudes. . . ."

At a table not far away the Hamlet of the evening was saying gloomily:

"Her mannerisms! Of course people like it just *at first*—but what I say is, it's not *Shakespeare.* Did you see how she ruined my exit?"

Nadine, sitting opposite Ginevra, said: "How exciting it is to be here in London with Jinny acting Ophelia and being so famous!"

Ginevra said softly: "It was nice of you to come over."

"A regular family party," said Nadine, smiling as she looked round. Then she said to Lennox: "I think the children might go to the matinée, don't you? They're quite old enough, and they *do* so want to see Aunt Jinny on the stage!"

Lennox, a sane, happy-looking Lennox with humorous eyes, lifted his glass.

"To the newly-weds, Mr. and Mrs. Cope."

Jefferson Cope and Carol acknowledged the toast.

"The unfaithful swain!" said Carol, laughing. "Jeff, you'd better drink to your first love as she's sitting right opposite you."

Raymond said gaily: "Jeff's blushing. He doesn't like being reminded of the old days."

His face clouded suddenly.

Sarah touched his hand with hers, and the cloud lifted. He looked at her and grinned.

"Seems just like a bad dream!"

A dapper figure stopped by their table. Hercule Poirot, faultlessly and beautifully apparelled, his moustaches proudly twisted, bowed regally.

"Mademoiselle," he said to Ginevra, "*mes hommages.* You were superb!"

They greeted him affectionately, made a place for him beside Sarah.

He beamed round on them all and when they were all talking he leaned a little sideways and said softly to Sarah:

" *Eh bien,* it seems that all marches well now with *la famille Boynton!*"

" Thanks to *you!*" said Sarah.

" He becomes very eminent, your husband. I read to-day an excellent review of his last book."

" It's really rather good—although I say it! Did you know that Carol and Jefferson Cope had made a match of it at last? And Lennox and Nadine have got two of the nicest children —cute, Raymond calls them. As for Jinny—well, I rather think Jinny's a genius."

She looked across the table at the lovely face and the red-gold crown of hair, and then she gave a tiny start.

For a moment her face was grave. She raised her glass slowly to her lips.

" You drink a toast, madame?" asked Poirot.

Sarah said slowly:

" I thought—suddenly—of Her. Looking at Jinny, I saw —for the first time—the likeness. The same thing—only Jinny is in light—where She was in darkness. . . ."

And from opposite, Ginevra said unexpectedly:

" Poor mother . . . She was *queer.* . . . Now—that we're all so happy—I feel kind of sorry for her. She didn't get what she wanted out of life. It must have been tough for her."

Almost without a pause, her voice quivered softly into the lines from *Cymbeline* while the others listened spell-bound to the music of them:

> " *Fear no more the heat o' 'the sun,*
> *Nor the furious winter's rages;*
> *Thou the worldly task hast done,*
> *Home art gone, and ta'en thy wages. . . ."*